DEAR GOD

... Hear my prayer

Dear God

... Hear my prayer

This is a work of fiction. All names, places, events and etc. are a creation of the author's imagination. If there are any similarities, it is purely coincidental.

Dedication

This book, like all the rest, is dedicated to YOU! You are among the ones who continue to believe in me, book after book! Please don't stop. Your support and encouragement is the fuel I use to keep writing!

My Thanks

As always, I have to thank God for entrusting me with such an amazing gift. Each time I write, I am more grateful to Him for choosing this brown girl, the one society counted out, long ago, to carry a mantle some say I never would. Thank you God for the chance to prove them wrong and you right.

And to every person who encourages me, daily. My family, friends, social media and blog followers and to each of you who share my thoughts and posts. Most importantly, to those of you who pray for and support me. THANK YOU!

And to Angel Bearfield who always creates the most amazing book covers. May God never allow your creativity to run out.

If I had more pages, I'd name all of you. If I had longer arms, I'd hug each of you. If I had more time ... Instead, I'll simply say, THANK YOU!

August 17, 2002

"God is good Saints."

"Yes, He is. All the time." Members of the congregation yells.

I roll my eyes as I sit on the second pew, to the right, watching my stepdad prance in front of the people who fill the seats of Fellowship of Christ.

"He cleaned me up, took my feet out of the mess I was in and now I stand before you a changed man. Won't He do it?" He screams to the congregation that is up on their feet. "When I didn't know who I was, when I was in my sin, He didn't let me die. Amen church."

"Amen." My mom says waving her hands.

"I am a living witness of what God can do, what about you?" He asks. "The doors of the church are open. Will there be one?"

LATER THAT NIGHT

I hear the creaking of my bedroom door. I hurriedly close the book I'd been reading, by the moonlight, before sliding it under my pillow.

"Jayme."

My body stiffens at the sound of his voice.

"I know you're not asleep." He says snatching the cover from over my head.

"What do you want?"

"I was just checking on you." He sits down beside me. I slide over.

"Where is my mom?"

"She's asleep. You know how she gets when she takes that medicine. He puts his hand on my leg causing me to jump.

What are you doing?" I yell.

"Why are you so jumpy? I'm just checking on you."

"I'm fine, trying to go to sleep."

"Stop lying, I bet you were reading again."

Before I can react, he reaches under my pillow and snatches the book.

"What have I told you about lying to me?"

"It's just a book."

"And it's just a lie."

"Can you just give me my book, please?"

"I'll only give it back if you do something for me." He says.

"What?"

"Give me a kiss."

"That's okay, keep it." I tell him, crossing my arms.

"Here and stop acting like a child."

I refuse to reach for it so he lays it on my nightstand and just stands there.

"Can you please leave?" I ask him.

"Why do you treat me like this? You know I was just playing with you. You take stuff to serious." He sits back on the bed. "Jayme, you know I love you right?"

I shrug my shoulders.

"Little girl, when I married your mom, I moved y'all from that old, raggedy house you were staying in so you could have all this." He says waving his hand around. "Yet you act ungrateful and never say thank you."

"Thank you?"

"Yea, for everything I provide."

"My mom takes--"

"Your mom doesn't do anything." He says with the tone of his voice changing. "I do all of this. From the MP3 player to the shoes and all the clothes you have in that closet is because of me and not your mother!"

"James–"

"What have I told you about calling me by my first name?" He bends over and grabs my chin. "What is my name?"

I don't say anything.

"WHAT.IS.MY.NAME?"

"Daddy."

He kisses me on the lips.

"Uh, stop! What are you doing?"

"Teaching you how to be obedient. You know what the bible says. Now, give daddy a kiss."

A tear is sliding down my face as he put his cheek close to me. I slowly lean forward and when I am near him, he turns and I end up kissing him on the lips. He smiles.

"Good girl."

I slide back under the cover, squeezing my eyes shut hoping he leaves. When I hear my door close, I relax but then he snatches the covers back, pulling me to the edge of the bed.

I scream but he covers his mouth.

"Shut up!"

"Don't!"

His hand presses harder against my mouth.

"Shh," he says sliding my gown up. "It is God's will for me to turn you into a woman."

I begin to squirm and cry.

"Please don't do this."

He snatches my panties off and smells them. When he places his hand on my private part, I try to kick him but his legs have me penned.

"Stop fighting Jayme, it'll be over soon."

Chapter 1

"Mom, did you hear what I said." Jace screams.

"No baby, I'm sorry. What did you say?" I ask snapping out of my thoughts.

"I was telling you about my field trip tomorrow."

"Oh, your field trip huh? Sounds like someone is excited to be going to the Children's Museum."

"You coming, right?"

"It's you are and of course, I wouldn't miss it."

"Cool."

"Now, go to bed and I'll come tuck you in."

"Mom, I am eight years old. I don't need you to tuck me in."

"Well excuse me. Can I at least check on you before I go to bed?"

"Yea, that'll be alright." He shrugs.

"Boy bye with your grown self."

After I finish cleaning the kitchen and checking on Jace, who is reading, I spend the quiet time straightening up the front of the house before pouring a glass of wine. Grabbing my kindle from the table, I settle on the couch.

Sometime later, I hear knocking on the door. I look at the time and it's after eleven. Another knock.

I lay my kindle on the table and walk over to the window. When I look out and see who it is, I turn away.

"I'm only going to keep knocking so you may as well open the door Jayme."

I let out a sign and snatch it open. "What are you doing here?"

"Is that any way to greet a guest?" He says pushing his way in.

"You're not a guest. What do you want?"

"What I've always wanted, you."

"You need to leave."

He takes off his suit jacket and begins loosening his tie before turning to close and lock the door.

"What are you doing? Get out of my apartment."

"Where is Jace?" He asks.

"None of your business. How did you find us?"

"Did you think it would be hard, especially in my city?"

"James, just leave us alone."

"You know I can't do that. You're mine and you will always be mine."

"If you don't leave, I'm calling the police."

When I turn to get my phone from the table, he grabs me by the arm.

"You, of all people should know, I am not scared of the police!" He says pulling my head towards his face. "Hmm, you smell good."

"Let me go!"

"Do you really want to fight me? I mean, I don't mind because the more you fight, the more turned on I get."

"You're hurting me."

"I wouldn't have too if you were to act right. I know you've missed me."

"Please don't do this." I say, voice cracking.

"Don't do what? Take what's rightfully mine? Tears begin to fall.

"Please don't start the tears, they mess with your gag reflex. Now get it together because I have about 30 minutes before I need to get home."

He pushes me down on the couch, unzipping his pants and freeing himself. "See, he missed you." I try to jump up but he grabs me by my hair causing me to scream out.

"Jayme, please don't make me hurt you." He says squeezing my hair tighter.

"James, please don't do this. You know my son is here."

"Then you need to play nice." He whispers in my ear before putting one hand on the back of my head and slapping me on the jaw with the other. I look up at him. "You know how I like it."

He slides his penis into my mouth.

"Good girl." He says rubbing the side of my face. "Aw, yeah, just like that."

When he's done, he pulls out and ejaculates all over my face.

"You know how to please daddy." He says fixing his pants. He bends over and kisses me on the forehead. "Don't forget to lock up. There are some bad people out there."

He grabs his jacket from the couch and walks toward the door.

"Oh Jayme," he stops. "It doesn't do you any good to move because I'll find you, I always do."

When he leaves, I remove my shirt to wipe my face before locking the door and barely making it to my bathroom to empty the contents of my stomach into the toilet. When I'm done, I sit there crying until I hear Jace calling my name.

"Mom, are you okay?" He asks knocking on the bathroom door.

"Yea, I'm good baby, go back to bed."

"You sure?"

"Yes, I'm sure. Go back to bed."

The next morning, I roll over cringing at the sun after not being able to sleep all night. My thoughts were consumed with plotting the many ways to kill that bastard over and over again.

I hear Jace moving about in his room so I get up and try to act as normal as possible. I prepare Jace's breakfast and pack his lunch while he gets dressed.

"You're still coming to my field trip right?" He asks walking into the kitchen.

"Yes baby, I'll be there."

Chapter 2

I walk into First Source, the call center where I work to Josh standing at my cubicle.

"Dang girl, who kept you up all night?"

"Nobody and why do you always think it has something to do with a man?"

"Because it's the only thing that has me looking like this the next morning." He laughs.

"Jayme, can I see you for a moment." My department manager asks interrupting. "Josh, don't you have some work to do?"

"Bye girl, Cruella is on the prowl this morning." He says before walking off

"Good morning Ms. Evelyn, you wanted to see me?" "Have a seat." She pulls out a folder. "Jayme, I'm going to cut to the chase. You're one of the best reps we have in this department but unfortunately, I'm going to have to let you go."

"What? Why?"

"I'm sorry but it's out of my control."

"Ms. Evelyn, whatever I've done, tell me what to do to fix it."

"Jayme, you haven't done anything but here's what you can do." She says pausing. "You can pack up your things and move to your new office because you're being promoted to Customer Service Manager."

"I, wait, what?"

"Congratulations."

"Ms. Evelyn, are you serious?"

"If anyone deserves this, it is you."

She hands me a sheet of paper and at the top, in bold letters are the words, Job Offer."

"Oh my God. Thank you Ms. Evelyn, this means so much."

"You don't have to thank me. Your work speaks highly of you and there is nobody better to handle this position."

"Thank you! Thank you!"

"Come on, I'll show you to your new office."

When we walk out of her office, my coworkers are there clapping and offering their congratulations.

"Girl, we drinking tonight." Josh whispers before Evelyn waves him off.

I spend the remaining of the morning moving the few things I had at my cubicle to my new office while still trying grasp what happened. My name plate has already been put up, making it official but it's still surreal.

Looking at my watch, I realize I'm running late for Jace's field trip so I turn off the light, lock the door and run out.

Rushing into the Children's Museum, I finally find Jace's class. I didn't have a chance to change shoes and walking around in four inch heels with a group of fourth graders is going to make for a long day.

After spending three hours with a bunch of hyperactive children, I am worn out. Jace comes running up to me. "Mom, can I spend the night at Josiah's house?"

"Well I will have to call Ms. Wanda."

"Oh it's fine." She says coming up behind me. "Hey Jayme, how are you?"

"I am good. I didn't know you were here?" I say giving her a hug

"I just got here. I was supposed to chaperone but my meeting ran over."

"Are you sure it's okay for him to spend the night?"

"Of course, it's all Josiah has been talking about."

"Then I guess that's a yes. I will take him by the house to get some clothes and then drop him off. Do you need me to bring anything?"

"Just Jace."

An hour later, I drop Jace off at Wanda's before stopping by a local beauty salon.

"Can I help you?" The receptionist ask.

"I don't have an appointment but I was hoping to get a haircut."

"Um," she says looking around. "Toya, can you take a walk-in?"

"Yea, send her back."

"Toya will be your stylist today. Go back to station three and she'll take care of you."

I thank her and walk back. I sit in the chair and she drapes a cape over me.

"Hey, my name is Toya. What do you need today?"

"A relaxer and cut."

"Okay, how short?"

"As short as possible."

"You sure?" She asks grabbing my hair that's hanging down my back.

"Very."

She nods and begins to work. Two hours later, I pay her and walk out with a short pixie cut. I rub my hand over the back of my head and although I'm going to miss my long hair, I think about James.

Nobody will ever be able to cripple me again!

I head home to change clothes because Josh will not let me back out on drinks tonight. I rarely go out but since I have something to celebrate and Jace is gone, what the heck. I shower and put on a jean jumper paired with a pair of black peep toe boots.

Pulling up at LOVE, a local club, I valet before walking in to find Josh. I decide to head to the bar, hoping I'll be able to see him from there.

"Jayme!" He yells out. "Okay Ms. Manager, I am loving this new you." He says twirling me around. "I didn't even know you had all this under the layers of clothes you normally wear to work."

"Shut up and buy me a drink."

"Already got you covered, we're in VIP and there's someone I want you to meet."

"Okay then, Mr. VIP, lead the way."

We walk up some stairs and through a roped off section, into VIP. Turning the corner, I see some familiar faces from work.

"Surprise!" They all shout.

I look back at Josh and he throws up his hands.

I take a few minutes to mingle and thank those who came out to help me celebrate.

Standing at the VIP bar, waiting on my drink, Josh slides him arm through mine.

"I want to introduce you to someone." He says with a wide smile. "And before you say anything, he's the one."

I look at him.

"I'm for real this time so don't be all up in my business with the questions."

"We shall see."

"Here he comes." He says swinging me around. "Jayme, meet my boyfriend--"

"Jackson." I say cutting him off.

"You know him?" Josh asks looking at me. When I don't say anything, he looks to Jackson. "You know her?"

"She's my sister." He says.

Chapter 3

"I have to go." I grab my clutch and walk as fast as I can, pushing through people trying to get down the steps and out of there.

Josh is on my trail and after I hand my ticket to the valet, he grabs my arm.

"Oh no heifer, you are not leaving without telling me what the hell just happened. Jackson is your brother, like DNA match type brother?"

"Unfortunately."

"You never told me you had a brother."

"Jayme," Jackson says walking up behind Josh. "Can we talk?"

"There's nothing to talk about. Josh, I'll see you Monday."

"Please." Jackson says. "Fifteen minutes."

I roll my eyes. "Fine."

"Can we can go to the Waffle House down the street?"

I hand the five dollar bill to the attendant.

"I'll wait for you." He yells to my back.

Against my better judgment, I finally convince myself to get out of my car and go inside Waffle House. When he sees me, he stands up.

"Thank you for meeting me."

"Don't thank me yet." I say sliding into the booth.

"It is good to see you Jayme. What has it been, five years since we've seen one another?"

"I guess."

"Can I get you something to drink, darling?" The waitress asks.

"Coffee please." My stomach growls reminding me I haven't eaten. "Can I go ahead and order too, please?"

"Whatcha having?"

"I'll take some eggs scrambled with cheese, raisin toast and hash browns, scattered, smothered and covered." I tell her.

"What ah bout you Suga?" She ask Jackson.

"I'll have the same thing but with orange juice."

When she leaves, Jackson begins to talk.

"I love the haircut."

"You have your dad to thank for it."

He doesn't look surprised.

"You knew he'd found me?" I ask him.

"No, well yeah, I guess."

"It's either you did or you didn't."

"It's not like that Jayme. We've been trying to find you but I had no idea he did."

"Right."

"You have to believe me."

"I do?"

"Jayme, I don't want to argue with you."

"Then why are we here because as far as I am concerned there is nothing we need to discuss that will not end in an argument."

"That's not fair Jayme."

I laugh. "Fair? What do you know about fairness? What's not fair is having my family turn their back on me."

"You were the one who left."

"You know why I left." I say trying not to be loud.

"I know but we could have made it work."

"Oh so we make molestation work now? Wow, who knew?"

"What was I supposed to do?"

"Believe me! It was bad enough not to have my own mother believe me but my baby brother too."

"I did believe you but he's my father Jayme."

"That I am well aware of. Look, is this what you wanted to talk about?"

"Mom is sick." He blurts.

"And?"

"She is your mother."

"No, she's your mother because my mother turned her back on me the minute she chose her husband and the grandness of her life."

"But she's sick."

I shrug my shoulders.

"Will you at least come to see her? She's at home and being taken care of through hospice."

"Does he know you're gay?"

"No and don't change the subject."

"I'm not changing the subject, I'm ignoring it, big difference."

"Jayme, the doctors are only giving her six months. I know you're upset but it's been what, eight, nine years since you left? Can you just get over it and forgive her? Don't let her die with things this way. You'll regret it."

"JUST.GET.OVER.IT." I slowly repeat. "Do you know how long I've tried to get over it? Do you know how many nights I lay in bed trying to get the thoughts of what he did out of my head? Or how I wish I can remove these scars from my wrists? Do you? If only it were that easy but I guess you'd never understand being the gay son of a pastor and all."

The waitress sits our drinks down.

"I do."

"You do what?"

"I understand."

I look up from my coffee cup.

"Oh, he got you too, huh?"

He quickly wipes the tear from his face. "This isn't about me. Mom is dying and you need to see her."

"Why did you stay?"

He doesn't say anything.

I chuckle. "Money."

"What else am I supposed to do? It was only a few times and he hasn't touched me in years."

"Wow. Just when I think this family can't get any sicker. Y'all deserve each other."

I grab my purse to leave.

"Jayme, please don't go."   .

"Baby brother, it is obvious there is nothing else for us to talk about. Good luck to you."

Chapter 4

I get to my car and it will not start.

"Damn it!" I say hitting the steering wheel. "Please don't do this to me tonight." I try it a few more times and it finally cranks.

I make the fifteen minute drive to my apartment. Walking inside, I lock the door and drag myself to my bedroom. I turn the TV on and throw the remote on the bed while I undress.

"This is for somebody out there who is living with the thoughts of what molestation took from you. Beloved, you've got to forgive." The TV Evangelist says.

"Are you freaking kidding me?"

"God is waiting on you to make the first step. Will you? No matter what has happened, will you trust God to bring you out? All it takes is a little faith. Will you trust God?"

I grab the remote and turn the TV off.

"Trust God? Ha, that's funny. How in the hell am I supposed to trust "God"," I say using my fingers to make air quotes. "Trust God, they say. He'll protect you, they say. He'll be there for you, they say. But where were you God! Huh? Where were you when I needed you? When I was being molested and abused? Where were you?" I scream.

I fall into the floor. "Where were you?"

TWO WEEKS LATER

Taking a vacation day from work, I walk Jace to his bus stop and wait. After they leave, I decide to take a walk around the apartments. It was the end of September so the weather was nice and I needed the time to think of a way to get me and Jace away from Memphis.

Making it back to my apartment, I find James standing there.

"What do you want?"

"We need to talk."

"There is nothing we need to talk about."

"Look, you need to watch your mouth when talking to me. Now, open the door to this little income based apartment before I smack the hell out of you"

"No." I say folding my arms. "You need to leave."

"And if I don't. Do you really want to try me?" He asks walking up on me.

"Jayme, are you alright?" My neighbor asks walking out of her apartment.

I look at her. "Yeah, he was just leaving."

"I'll be back." He says rubbing his fingers over my lips. "And I love the haircut, it fits you.

I slap his hand from my face and wait until I am sure he's gone before opening my door.

Once inside, I grab my computer and begin to search for places that offer self-defense classes.

After jotting down a few, I get up to shower.

Walking out the bathroom tying my robe, I look up to see him sitting on my bed. I turn to run back into the bathroom but he's at the door before I can get it closed.

He pushes the door, causing me to fall back onto the floor.

"Did you honestly think I would leave?" He says pulling me up by the throat. I struggle to get his hand loose as it begins to be hard to breathe.

"Why do you insist on playing with me?"

I try again to pry his hands from around my neck.

"Stop," I barely get out.

He pushes me against the wall and loosens his grip.

"Now, apologize."

When I don't say anything, he raises his hand and I flinch.

"Now Jayme!"

"I'm sorry."

He stands in front of me and smiles while opening my robe. "Why do you always make our meeting so hard? I only came to talk to you but when you fight, it turns me on. Damn, you're gorgeous." He rubs his hand over my breast and down my stomach. "You were so beautiful when you carried my son, I think it's time we try for a little girl?"

His hand stops at the top of my vagina. "Please don't." I cry pushing his hand away.

He steps back and slaps me across my face, I fall onto the counter. He walks up behind me, spreading my legs while unzipping his pants, allowing them to drop to his ankles.

"What's my name?"

He places his hand around my neck.

"What's my name?" He ask again squeezing harder.

"Daddy." I cry.

"Good girl," he says before forcefully inserting himself into me. I cry out from the pain.

He puts one hand over my mouth and one on my shoulder. I cry into his hand from the pain between my legs but he doesn't stop. After a few minutes, his moans get a little louder and he collapses onto me, kissing my back.

He steps away, taking the towel from the towel rack before walking over to the sink, with his pants still down. I stand there and watch him clean himself up.

"What did I ever do to deserve this?" I ask him.

"What makes you think you did anything?"

"Then why? Why hurt me?"

"I'm not hurting you Jayme. I'm only getting use out of what belongs to me."

"I don't belong to you."

He laughs. "Of course you do, ask your mom."

"What do you mean?"

He doesn't answer and he fixes his clothes. "Your mother is sick. You need to come and see her before she dies. Oh, get out of this hell hole because your neighbors are too nosey." He pulls some money from his wallet and throws it on the sink before walking over to grab my chin again.

He kisses my on the lips. "I think I'll go and have lunch with Jace today. You know, just a little insurance to make sure you keep your mouth closed, this time."

"Leave my son out of this. I won't say anything."

He laughs before walking out.

When I finally hear the door close, I slide down to the floor.

"Dear God, please hear my prayer."

Chapter 5

"Can I help you?"

"I need to get the Plan B pill." I tell the pharmacy tech, pulling my sweater tighter.

She leaves and after a few minutes, she comes back. "Do you have any questions for the pharmacist?"

I shake my head no while handing her the bottle of water I'd picked up.

"That will be $42.75."

I insert my debit card. Completing the transaction, I take the receipt and bag from her.

As soon as I get into the car, I take out the pill and read the instructions before I swallow it with the water. Sitting there for a few more minutes, I pull out my phone and tap in the address of the nearby gym I found that offers self-defense classes.

Pulling up to Wallace Training Academy, I get out.

"How can I help you?"

"Uh, I am interested in a self-defense class."

"Have you ever been here before?"

"No."

"Well, welcome to Wallace Training Academy. My name is Jacob. First, I'll need you to fill out this information form. When you're done, I'll give you a tour of the facility and then we can discuss your options."

"Sounds great."

He shows me over to a computer in the corner. Once I am done, he leads me through the facility explaining the different things they offer.

"We specialize in all kinds of training but our biggest class is self-defense. Right this way." He leads me into an office and pulls out a chair for me to sit in.

"Now," he stops to look at my form I'd filled out. "Jayme, tell me what you're looking for. I know you said self-defense but are you needing extensive training or just enough to get someone off of you."

"What's the difference?"

"With the extensive training, you'll be trained well enough to kill someone with your bare hands. The regular--"

"I want the extensive."

"Okay. The price for this kind of training can normally run in excess of five hundred dollars but this month, it's on sale for $200.

"Sign me up."

"Great. I will have my assistant, Simone get you set up. I look forward to working with you Jayme."

I finish the necessary paperwork to get enrolled for Monday's class. Leaving the gym, I stop by Academy Sports to purchase some work out gear. Getting home, I leave the door cracked for Jace who should be coming in from school. After a few minutes, he walks in and drops his backpack by the door before slamming it and turning to walk to his room.

"Whoa partner, hold up. What's wrong with you?"

"Nothing."

"Jace, come here."

He walks over to me and it looks like he's been crying.

"What's wrong with you? Did something happen on the bus?"

He doesn't say anything as he bawls his hands up into fist.

"Jace, talk to me. What happened?"

"Why did granddaddy hurt you?"

The words get caught in my throat.

"That night, why did he do that to you?"

"You, um, you saw – what did you see?"

"I heard you scream so I got up and –– why would he hurt you?" He says as tears flow from his eyes.

I grab him and pull him into my chest matching my tears with his.

He sits up. "He came to my school today and I told him not to hurt you again."

"You did?" I ask wiping his face. "What did he say?"

He stands and lifts his shirt where a huge bruise is on his side.

"Oh my God! He did that to you?" I slide down to the floor and rub his side before I place my head on his stomach, crying. "I am so sorry. Please forgive me. Oh God, please forgive me."

He wraps his arms around me and I can feel him crying and it breaks my heart but more than anything, it makes me angry. I push him away so that I can look into his eyes.

"He will never hurt you again. Do you hear me? I will never allow him to hurt you again."

He nods his head before I hug him again.

"Maybe we can pray and ask God."

I look at him.

"What do you know about praying?"

"Ms. Wanda prays and she taught me how. Don't be mad."

Tears are starting to flow again.

"I'm sorry." He says.

"No, baby, I am not mad. I am glad Ms. Wanda taught you about God because it's been a long time since I have talked to him. Maybe you can teach me."

He gets down on his knees in front of the couch and motions for me to join him.

"Put your hands like this." He says clasping his hands together in front of his face. "Close your eyes."

He then begins praying, "Dear God, thank you for another day. Thank you for my momma, Ms. Wanda, Josiah and my teacher. Bless us and keep us safe. Protect my mom and please don't let my granddaddy hurt us again. Amen."

Chapter 6

Monday

Leaving work, I pick Jace up from the bus stop before we stop by Chick Fil A for an earlier dinner and head to the gym.

"Hey, are you here for tonight's class?"

"Yes."

"Did you download the app?"

"I did." I say pulling out my phone.

"Great, I will show you how to check in.

Once I am checked in, I put my phone into my purse.

"You are all checked in. The class will begin in ten minutes. Do you remember where the locker rooms are?" Simone asks.

"Yes but is there an area where my son can do his homework?"

"We have a play area but we don't–"

"He can use my office."

I turn to see Jacob.

"Are you sure?"

"Of course." He says before turning to Jace. "Hi, I'm Jacob."

"I'm Jace. Are you a boxer?"

"Oh no. I'm a police officer."

"You are?" Jace asks as his eyes light up.

"I sure am and if you come to my office, I'll show you."

"Bye mom!"

I laugh at how fast Jace took off behind Jacob. I walk into the women's locker room and change clothes. Standing in front of the mirrors, I look at myself in the mirror trying to calm my nerves.

I walk out and the room is filled with women.

"Okay ladies, are you ready to learn how to kick some butts?" Jacob asks.

"Yes."

"Oh come on now. You can give me a better yes than that. Are you ready to learn how to kick some butts?"

"YES!" We all yell.

"Good. Let's go."

Over the next hour, we spend time stretching and learning the basic aspects of self-defense. When we are done, I am sweating and so out of breathe that I have to sit on the floor for a moment.

Jacob walks over to me.

"You did great tonight."

"Thank you. You are a great instructor, hard but still great."

"I hope I didn't work you too hard that you decide not to come back."

"Oh, I'll definitely be back."

"Great, then I will see you on Wednesday."

I grab my things from the locker room before going to find Jace. When I get to the office door, I hear him talking.

"Are you going to help my mom?"

"Help your mom with what?"

"Help her learn how to fight?"

"I am going to try." Jacob says.

"Good because she needs it."

"She does? Who does she need to fight?"

"My granddad, he hurts her."

"Jace, are you ready?" I ask walking into the room.

"Yes ma'am."

"Jayme, is everything okay?" Jacob asks.

"Everything is fine."

"If you need help, please don't be afraid to tell me. I am a member of the Memphis Police Department and I can help."

"I am good but thank you."

"Here is my card and if there is anything you need, don't hesitate to call me. Here little man, you take one too."

I grab Jace's backpack before pushing him out the room.

"Why would you tell him that?" I ask after getting into the car.

"It's true."

"It maybe but you cannot go around telling my business. Listen, I know you're scared but I will not let James hurt us again."

He sighs. "Okay."

Getting home, I send Jace to take his bath while I lock up and head to do the same. Once we are done, I check on him and climb into bed. I am so tired, I don't even bother turning on the TV.

Some hours later, I am jolted from my sleep at the sound of glass breaking. I grab my phone and jump up. I slowly walk to my bedroom door before running down to Jace's room. He jumps when I open the door.

"What's happening?"

"Shh, I don't know. Come to me." I take his hand and we squeeze into his closet.

"Memphis 911, what is your emergency?"

"Someone is breaking into my home?"

"What's your address?"

"7454 Gold Avenue, apartment two."

"Is there anyone else in the home with you?"

"Just my son."

"Can I have your name?"

"Jayme Walker."

"Okay Ms. Walker, officers are three minutes out. Stay on the line."

After what seems like forever, I hear officers calling my name. Jace and I get come out the closet and I let them know where we are.

"Ma'am, are you okay?'

"Yes." I say shaking.

"We cleared your home and didn't find anybody. It doesn't look as if someone broke in but there was a brick thrown through your window. Come with me?"

"Jace, stay here." I hand him my phone.

I follow him to the living room and see a brick laying on the floor.

"Do you have any idea who would do this?"

"No." I say pacing.

"We can get crime scene out to try and lift prints, if you are willing to file a report."

"Yes, I definitely am willing."

He goes outside and I go into my bedroom to change out of my night clothes. By the time I make it back to the living room, Jacob is coming through the door.

"Jayme, are you and Jace okay?"

"How, what are you doing here?"

"Jace called me."

The other officer comes in and he steps to the side to talk to Jacob. When they are done, he begins to ask questions in order to fill out the report. I notice Jacob as he goes into Jace's room.

By the time I am done with answering all the needed questions, a crime scene officer comes and removes the brick.

"Ma'am, your window isn't fully broken and it should hold until you can get someone out to fix it in the morning."

"Thank you officer."

"No problem ma'am. Have a great night."

I close the door and turn to Jacob.

"Jayme, are you sure you're okay?" He asks.

"Yes, we are fine now."

"Do—"

"Look, I don't mean to be rude but we are fine. I appreciate your concern but Jace should have never called you. The other officers took the report and I will have maintenance fix the window in the morning."

He hesitates before speaking. "I understand. Have a great night."

When he leaves, I lock the door before cleaning up the glass. Turning out the lights, I walk into my bedroom to find Jace sitting in the middle of my bed.

"Boy, you scared the crap out of me."

"Can I sleep with you tonight?"

"Yea but we need to talk."

"Are you mad I called Mr. Jacob?"

"Yes, no." I sigh. "Look Jace, I understand you were scared but you shouldn't have called him?"

"He said if we needed anything to call him. Ma, we needed him tonight."

"We needed the police."

"He is the police." He says.

"You know what, never mind, go to sleep."

"Wait, we need to say our prayers."

He hops down off the bed and kneels. "Come on."

I kneel next to him and close my eyes. When he doesn't say anything, I look at him. "What?"

"You do it?"

"Um, okay." I sigh. "Dear God, thank you for keeping me and my son safe. Thank you for watching over us. Please protect us because I cannot do it alone. I know I haven't talked to you in a while and no matter how hard I try not to, I still believe in you. Please show me what to do. Amen."

"And bless Mr. Jacob. Amen."

I cut my eye at him and he shrugs his shoulders.

"Boy, get your tail in the bed."

Chapter 7

It's been a few days since someone through a brick through my window. I spoke to a detective but there were no prints. I called my Department Manager, yesterday and explained everything that's going on and she approved for me to take some time off.

I hope this doesn't jeopardize my new promotion but this cannot be helped. I am already scheduled for a week of vacation during Fall Break, in a few weeks but I need to find me and Jace a new place to live now. I have a few apartments lined up that are within my price range and I am praying I can get something as soon as possible.

I roll over and pain shoots up my back. Jace has been afraid to sleep in his room, which means I haven't been sleeping well. I had the locks changed and the window fixed but it is still hard to feel safe.

I pry his legs from me as I get up to handle my morning hygiene. Before I can get up good, my phone vibrates. I grab it and walk into the bathroom.

"Hello."

"Why haven't you been to see your mother?"

"The same reason I've never been to see her."

"I don't know why you insist on playing with me. You either see her on your terms or mine."

I hang up the phone and block the number. I will not be forced to see a woman who never gave a damn about me. I'm sorry she's dying but that is between her and her God.

I finish in the bathroom and dress in some leggings, an oversize t-shirt and some fuzzy socks. Walking into the kitchen, I pull out bacon, eggs and pancake mix. Sitting a skillet on the stove, I turn it on and add a little oil when the doorbell rings.

I open it to find Jacob.

"What are you doing here?"

"I wanted to check on you and your son. I know how upset and scared he was the other night and I just wanted to make sure the both of you were okay. And I bought this for him." He says handing me a hand held game.

"That was kind of you but we're, he is fine."

"Have I done anything to you?" He asks.

"Other than overstep your boundaries?"

"I apologize if you think that but I only want to make sure you and your son are safe and that whoever hurt you before won't do it again."

"What did you say?"

"I saw the bruises around your neck the day you came into my gym and--"

The smoke detector starts to beep. I run into the kitchen but can't reach it. When I turn around, Jacob is standing there.

"Do you always come into people's houses uninvited?"

He doesn't say anything before reaching up to remove the smoke detector while I put the skillet in the sink and turn off the stove.

"Jacob, I appreciate your concern for my son but he's fine so you can stop checking up on us." I say snatching the smoke detector from his hand.

"I'll back off but the offer still stands. If there is ever anything you need, just call. Please give this to your son."

"Is this new?" I ask him.

"The game?"

"No, these home visits because I have never known police officers to do this so, please tell me what you really want?"

He shakes his head. "Have a great day." He turns to leave but stops. "I don't know what you've been through but I am not the bad guy."

"That's what they all say. Have a great day Officer Wallace."

"I noticed you don't have an alarm. You really should get one because it'll make you feel safer."

"Oh and what else have you noticed?" I ask crossing my arms. "Because I've noticed you all up in my business."

He shakes his head again.

"Why do you keep shaking your head? Is there something else you want to say?"

"No."

"Go on and say it. I mean, you may as well get it all off your chest."

"Okay, this conversation is not going the way I intended. I, again, apologize for coming here but I am not sorry for showing up the night your son called me. I thought I was doing a good thing but it's obvious you've been so hurt by men that you cannot see it. I'm sorry."

"Oh, I get it." I laugh. "Not only are you a police officer and self-defense instructor but you are also a therapist. Well, thank you Dr. Wallace for your diagnosis. Send me your bill and I'll file it on my insurance."

"I am not a therapist but it isn't hard to see you've been hurt. It's written all over your face and it is in your eyes but I will not apologize for what everybody else has done to you. I am not here for anything nor do I have an agenda. My mother and father raised me to respect women and it is also my job to serve and protect. I am sorry if that Is hard for you to believe but I will not bother you again."

"No, don't leave now when you've spent the last twenty minutes judging me."

"I am not judging you Jayme. I am just trying to help."

"Why though? What's in it for you? Yes, I've been hurt, probably more than you can ever imagine by men who look just like you."

"Just like me?"

"Yes, those who are well put together, sharp dressers with a fresh cut who are supposed to serve and protect. You start off by saying all the right things, being the perfect guy but all you men do is take, take, and take; never thinking about anybody but yourself. You want to know why I am the way I am? It's because my step daddy has been taking whatever he wanted from me since I was 14. You know what he's given me? A lifetime of misery and a son. So excuse me if my harsh tone and attitude offends you but it's all I got left."

"Granddaddy is my daddy?" Jace asks from behind me and my heart drops.

I turn to him. "Jace, I–"

He runs to his room and slams the door.

"Got damn it!" I scream. "What else do you want from me? Huh? What else? Haven't I been punished enough?"

I fall into the floor, crying. When Officer Wallace comes near me, it makes it worse. I begin swinging at him to push him away and it's the last thing I remember.

Chapter 8

I blink a few times before turning my head and bolting up in the bed.

"Hold on, take it easy."

"What happened?"

"You passed out. Here, there was some ibuprofen in your medicine cabinet." He says handing me four and a bottle of water."

"Where is my son?"

He's in his room.

"How long have you been here?"

"It doesn't matter, just take the pills."

I swallow the pills and sit the glass on the nightstand. "Why are you still here Officer Wallace? Don't you have a job and family of your own?"

"Call me Jacob and I wasn't about to leave you alone. Your son told me you didn't have any family so I decided to wait until you woke up. You've been out a while so I ordered a pizza but he didn't eat."

"Why?"

"He said he wasn't hungry."

"I meant, why are you still here?"

"You looked like you needed help."

"So, are you my knight in shining armor?"

"No, they don't exist. I am simply the guy God used at the right time."

"God? Yea okay."

"I was only trying to help."

"I DON'T NEED YOUR HELP!"

"What is wrong with you?"

"What's wrong with you?" I ask swinging my legs off the bed. "You don't know me from a stranger on the street and I damn sure don't know you but you're in my house, feeding my son and acting like, like – you know what? It doesn't matter. Thank you for everything but you need to go."

"Look Jayme. To be honest--",

"Here it comes."

He shakes his head. "To be honest, I don't know why I felt the need to come here this morning but it's not to take advantage of you, that I am sure of. Although, I cannot begin to know all you've been through, one thing is for sure, I am not the enemy."

"Just go, please."

He stands up. "I will but if you need anything or want someone to talk to, you can call me."

I wait until I hear the front door close before I get up and make sure the door is locked. Walking into my bathroom, I turn on the water to shower. Undressing and stepping inside, I slide down onto the floor.

"Dear God, why are you allowing these things to happen to me? Whatever it is, I have done, I am sorry. Please forgive me and stop this pain. I'll go back to church, I'll pray more and if I have to go and see my mother, I will but please; I don't know how much more I can take. I need you to help me because I'm lost and I can't do it by myself anymore. Please God, hear my prayer."

I sit there until the water gets cold before getting out and putting on my robe.

Sighing, I go into Jace's room. He has his face toward the wall. I grab his remote and turn down the volume on the TV before touching him on his arm. When he looks back at me, I can tell he's been crying.

"Jace, we need to talk." I tell him pulling a chair next to his bed. He slowly turns over to face me.

"I hate him." He screams. "I hate him for hurting you. I'll kill him!"

I grab him, pulling him into my lap as he screams and cry. "I hate him."

"I'm so sorry baby. I never meant any of this for you."

"I'll protect you." He sobs.

"No baby, I'm going to protect you."

"I don't want you to hate me." He cries.

"Why would I hate you?"

"Because he's my dad."

"Oh baby, I can never hate you. You're my only son and you mean everything to me. When I had you, you saved me. I can never hate you."

He cries and hugs me tighter.

I rock him in my arms until he cries himself to sleep. I lay him back in his bed, putting him under the cover.

I put his chair back before sliding down on the floor in front of his dresser. Watching him sleep, I silently cry for the pain he's feeling, for the anger growing in his belly and for his innocence been shattered. And I cry for failing my son.

"Dear God, I surrender."

Chapter 9

THE NEXT DAY

Jace and I spend the entire day hanging out at the movies, the mall and somehow he talked me into taking him to Sky Zone. I smile when I pull in the driveway and look in the rear view mirror to see him asleep in the back seat.

"Jace baby, come on we're home."

Getting out the car, we walk to the front door to find it open again.

Pushing the door open, "How did you get in here?"

"What do you want?" Jace yells at James who is sitting on the couch.

"Boy, you'd better lower your voice."

"HOW.DID.YOU.GET.IN.MY.HOUSE?" I ask through clinched teeth.

"I have my ways." He smiles.

"Jace, go to your room."

"No, I'm not leaving you."

"I'll be alright. I promise."

"We don't want you here!" Jace screams at James.

"Son, I know you're upset but you need to remember who you're talking too. You better watch that smart mouth of yours before--"

"I dare you to lay another hand on him." I say pushing Jace behind me. "Get the hell out of my house."

He starts to laugh. "Little girl, you do not want to play with me."

"I am not a little girl anymore and after these past few weeks, I can promise you don't want to try me so leave before one of us ends up in a body bag and the other in jail."

He walks toward me. "Is that a threat?"

"No, it's a promise."

He stops right next to me. "You better go and see your mother. You have until the end of the week or that brick through your window will be the least of your worries."

"That was you?"

"Just keeping you on your toes."

"You're sick."

"I'll be back." He says smiling.

"And I'll be waiting."

After he leaves, I lock the door.

"Jace baby, go and pack a bag. We aren't staying here tonight."

I go into my bedroom and pack a small bag, only grabbing the essential things I need. Once Jace is done, I lock up and head to the nearest hotel.

Once we are checked in, we walk across the parking lot to the Waffle House to eat. Getting back to our room, I sit on the bed while Jace takes a bath.

I open the drawer and see a bible.

"They still put bibles in hotels?" I say to myself while flipping through it. "Okay God, I need you to show up. I don't know if you will but if you're there, show me."

I put the bible on the bed when I hear Jace coming out the bathroom. I grab my clothes and go in after him.

When I am done, I come out to see him on his bed with the bible.

"What are you doing?"

"Reading."

"The bible? What do you know about the bible?"

"Ms. Wanda says there are a lot of great stories in here. Did you know that?"

"I did."

"Do you think we can read it together sometimes?"

"Sure."

"And maybe we can start going to church with Josiah and Ms. Wanda. He always tells me about the things he learns and it sounds fun."

"Um, I don't know Jace but maybe."

"Why? Don't you believe in God?"

"I do but it's complicated."

"Well Ms. Wanda says God loves all of us and He is always there."

"Ok, bible scholar, it's time for you to go to sleep because you have school in the morning."

"Okay but we have to say our prayers."

We both kneel beside the bed and this time Jace prays. When he is done, he gets under the covers.

"Ma?"

"Yes Jace."

"I love you and God loves you too."

I smile at him. "I know and I love you too."

I turn out the lights and I try not too but I can't help but cry. When I think of all the things that have gone wrong in my life, having Jace has been, by far, the best thing to ever happen.

I close my eyes.

"Jayme."

"Hmm?"

"Jayme."

I open my eyes to a figure I can't make out. I jump up.

"You don't have to be afraid."

"Who are you? What do you want?"

"You ask me to show up. Here I am."

"What? Who are you?"

"Tonight, when you were holding my word in your hands, didn't you ask me to show up?"

I laugh, "This can't be real? I'm tripping."

"Don't you believe in me? I believe in you."

"Yea right? Why should I believe in you, after everything I've been through? Why didn't you save me?"

"I did."

"What?"

"I did save you or you wouldn't be here today?"

"Then you should have let me die because living like this is no way to live."

"Says who?"

"Me!" I yell. "Why didn't you stop it? All those nights I cried while my stepdad did any and everything to me, where were you?"

"I was there."

"I am done with this game or whatever it is because I remember and you were not there."

"If you close your eyes, you'd see I was right there with you through everything. Those nights you were balled up in the corner of your closet, I was there holding you. Those times you tried to commit suicide, I was there stopping it.

Those moments when you wanted to give up, it was I that strengthened you to go on. My beloved. I didn't forsake you, I was just silent during your test."

"What test?"

"The test of your faith. I didn't allow you to go through all those things for punishment, I did in order that you might see my promise for your life. My promise to give you a future and a hope. My promise to prosper you, not harm you."

"And you expect me to believe that molestation is a test?"

"No daughter but there are some people who are evil and who seek to destroy those who believe in me. Some of those are people who do work in my name."

"Why don't you stop them?"

"I will but until then I need you to trust me."

"I don't know how."

"It starts by believing I'll protect you." "Why does it have to hurt so badly?"

"My daughter, the size of your purpose determines the amount of your pain."

"Well, when will it end?" I ask.

"In due time but I need you to trust me. Will you?"

"It's hard."

"Will you try?"

Yes."

"That's all I need. Now, go to your mother."

"Why?"

"For closure."

"Mom, mom; wake up."

"What?"

"I have school, remember?" Jace says standing there fully dressed.

I sit up and look around. It felt like I'd just gone to sleep and now ... this couldn't have been real.

"What time is it?"

"7:05."

Chapter 10

I drop Jace off at school before making the 25 minute drive to Tipton County. I don't know why but after that dream last night, I felt the need to see my mom.

I pull into the driveway of the massive home belonging to James and Josephine Madison, Tipton County's most deceptive power couple.

"If only people knew the secrets behind those doors." I say into the air.

After sitting there a few minutes, I finally get out. I ring the doorbell and a lady dressed in scrubs answers.

"Can I help you?" She asks.

"Yes, I'm here to see Josephine Madison."

"Is she expecting you?"

"Nope."

"Your name?"

"Jayme."

"Wait here while I speak to Mrs. Madison."
She says stepping back to let me in.

After a few minutes, she comes back.

"Follow me."

She leads me down the hallway to a set of
doors. She taps on the door before pushing it
open.

"Go on," she says when my feet wouldn't move.

I walk in and see my mother sitting up in a hospital bed with a scarf wrapped around her head and a face full of makeup.

"Not bad for someone dying." I say standing at the foot of her bed.

"I didn't expect to see you again in this lifetime?"

"Hello Josephine."

"Did you came to see if it was true?"

"To be honest mother, I only came for closure."

"Oh, you're expecting an apology or something."

"No Josephine because that would be too much like right but answer something for me."

"What?"

"Why did you allow James to do those things to me?"

She shrugs her shoulders before taking a sip of water.

"What did I ever do to you Josephine? I am your only daughter yet I wasn't good enough to love. Why not?"

"I do love you."

I laugh, wiping the tears falling from my eyes. "And you couldn't find another way to show me other than letting your husband have his way with me? All I ever wanted was for you to protect me."

"Nobody protected me!" She says getting louder. I look at her. "Oh, you thought you were the only one who has ever had something taken from you? When I was thirteen, he started coming into my room having his way with me. Even when my screams filled the little house we stayed in, my mother never came. You know what she did? She closed her bedroom door. See, as long as daddy was getting what he needed from me, he didn't have to get it from her. She told me to suck it up."

"Even more reason for you to protect me."

"You didn't need protecting, you needed to be quiet. James was only making you into a woman."

"No mother, he made me wounded."

"You look like you survived to me."

"What does James mean when he says I owe him?"

"How do you think we got to live as well as we did?"

"Wow. I was your sacrificial lamb?"

"Sometimes you have to make a deal with the devil."

"Goodbye Josephine."

"Wait," she says. "You ought to know what I'm dying from."

"Why? It doesn't matter to me."

"That's where you're wrong dear. I have AIDS."

My eyes widen. "You, you have what?"

"AIDS. And there is nothing more I want them to do. I'm tired of living in this hell hole."

"James?"

"Who do you think I got it from? I guess this is what happens when the devil comes to collect."

The door opens and the nurse comes in.

"You might want to get checked sweetie. Now, if you'd leave me, it's time for my nap."

I turn to leave and then stop.

"I hope you get the punishment you deserve in the next life that you never got in this one."

"I have no doubt I will." She says.

Making it to my car, I pull off. The tears are pouring from my eyes making it hard to see, so I pull over and scream like it's the last thing I'd ever do before beginning to beat the steering wheel.

"Dear God, why did you send me here?"

I grip the steering wheel before laying my head on it. Someone knocking on my window causes me to jump.

I let the window down.

"Ma'am, are you okay?" The officer says.

I try to talk but the only thing that comes out is moans.

"Are you hurt? Do you need an ambulance?"

When I still don't answer, she goes to grab her radio and I stop her. She reaches in and unlocks the door. Opening it, she does something unexpected. She unbuckles my seatbelt and wraps her arms around me, letting me cry.

"I don't know what you're dealing with beloved but God has you. This battle you're fighting, it isn't punishment but it's positioning you for something greater." She says while rocking me. "Dear God, whatever it is, fix it. Whatever the past did, remove it because I declare victory sweet Jesus, by the blood of your Son on Calvary. Clean and restore her giving her a brand new heart. Come now God because your daughter is crying out to you. Incline your ear and meet her need. Please dear God, hear her prayer. Amen."

After a few minutes, she releases me.

"Are you okay?"

"I, um, I don't know what to say. Thank you."

"You don't have to thank me. I am here to serve and protect and that doesn't always mean from criminals." She steps back and closes the door. "God hasn't forsaken you, no matter how hot the fire gets."

"Who are you?" I laugh while wiping my face.

"My name is Officer Mia Stewart and even while I am in this uniform, I proudly wear the uniform of being God's servant. Here's my card. If you're ever in the area, I'd love for you to visit God's church where my husband is Sr. Pastor."

"Thank you Officer Stewart. I am Jayme, by the way."

"I know, you're the Madison's daughter. It's nice to see you Jayme. Take care and be safe."

"I definitely will."

Just then another car pulls over on the opposite side of the street.

"Jayme?"

When I hear his voice I jump.

"Officer Stewart, is everything okay?" He asks her walking across the two lane road.

"Mr. Madison, everything is fine. Why do you ask?" She turns but never leaves the door. It's almost like she is blocking him from getting to me.

"That's my daughter."

She turns back to look at me. I shake my head no.

"Mr. Madison, she is fine. If you can get back in your vehicle please."

"I'm not leaving until I know what in the hell is going on?"

She turns to me. "Be safe getting home."

I smile at her one last time and pull off.

Chapter 11

When I make it back to the hotel, I sit in the chair looking at my phone dreading the call I knew I had to make. Taking a deep breathe, I dial the number.

Putting the phone to my ear, a tear slides down as she answers.

"Um yes, I need to make an appointment. Jayme, J-A-Y-M-E Walker. 5/17/90."

She pauses as she searches for me in the system.

"Yes, um, I need to be tested for HIV. Yes, ok, thank you."

Hanging up, I cry. I am so sick of crying but I've never been more hurt in my life. What in the hell will I do if I have HIV? What happens if I die? Who will take care of my son? All of these questions swirl through my head as I go to lie down on the bed.

The vibrating of my phone wakes me. It's a text from an unknown number. I look at the time and realize I've overslept.

I quickly jump up and grab my purse. When I open the door, James is standing there.

"Why do you insist on defying me?"

"How did you find me?"

"Didn't I tell you, I'd always find you?"

"Look, I don't have time for this."

I try to push pass him but he grabs me.

"I need to go and get my son."

"You will leave when I say you can."

He pushes me into the room and closes the door.

"What did you tell Officer Stewart?"

"What? I didn't tell her anything."

"Stop lying!" He yells. "What did you say to her?"

He slaps me causing me to fall onto the nightstand.

"I'm going to ask you one last time, what did you say to her?"

I grab the bottle of Cranberry Apple juice I had last night and hit him on the side of his head. When he falls against the bed, I swing again but he raises his hand, so it connects with his wrist.

I drop the bottle and run out.

Making it to my apartments, I pull up and park before jumping out to find Jace. I was over 30 minutes late and it's cold.

Running to my apartment, I don't see him.

"Jace!" I yell starting to panic. "Jace."

I take out my phone and another call is coming through from Wanda.

"Hello. Oh my God! Thank you. I am on the way." I let out a breath when she tells me Jace is with her. I get into my car and before I can get to Wanda's, there is a police car behind me with its lights on.

I pull over and let my window down.

"Officer, did I do something wrong?"

"License please."

I reach into my wallet and hand it to him before asking again what I did wrong. I know I wasn't speeding.

"Ma'am, I need you to step out of the car."

"Why? What did I do?"

"Step out of the car ma'am, now."

I unfasten my seat belt and open the door. He snatches me out.

"What did I do?"

"Ms. Walker, you are under arrest."

"Under arrest? For what?"

"Please turn around."

"Can I--"

"Ma'am, turn around."

He places me in handcuffs and leads me to the police car. I see another officer taking the keys from the ignition and locking the door.

Making it to the police station, I am put into an interrogation room where I stay for over 2 hours.

"Ms. Walker, my name is Detective Eddie Lewis. Do you know why you're here?"

"I sure don't and it has to be against the law to hold somebody without telling them what they are under arrest for."

"You're being charged with aggravated assault."

"On?"

"James Madison. Would you like to give your side of the story?"

"Wow, okay. My side? Obviously James Madison has connections otherwise I wouldn't be sitting here and it hadn't even been an hour.

There is no way you could have gotten an arrest warrant that quick."

"So you admit to assaulting the victim?"

"Oh, he's the victim?"

"Ma'am, you're the one sitting here, not him."

"Are you a member of his church?"

"This is not about me? And if you don't tell your side of the story, you'll be spending the night in jail."

"I doubt that."

"Okay, you want to play tough? Fine."

"Can I make a phone call? I need to check on my son."

He slides me his cell phone.

"Make it quick."

I dial Wanda's number. I give her as much information as I can and ask her to watch Jace for me. When I release the call, I give him the phone back.

"How do you know James?" I ask him.

He looks at me. I laugh.

"He has you fooled too, huh?"

"Ma'am, what happened between you and Mr. Madison?"

'He showed up at my room, attacked me and I fought back."

"Why didn't you stay at the scene?"

"Because I had to pick up my son. I was already running late."

"Why would Mr. Madison attack you?"

"He's a monster but I'm sure that's hard for you to believe."

"Why should I believe a pillar of the community, an upstanding man of God who is heavily involved in the affairs of this city would attack you, for nothing."

"I didn't say it was for nothing."

"Then why would he attack you?"

"To keep his secrets buried."

"What secrets?"

"Come on Detective, you are not blind and I am sure you've heard the rumors about him. It's quite obvious you don't believe them but that's your choice."

He chuckles. "Are you really willing to ruin a man's reputation? Come on Ms. Walker, what's the real story."

"Detective Lewis, I am done talking to you. Either charge me or let me go."

He leaves out and I am left sitting there again. When the door opens this time, it is another officer who takes me to an area and places me in a cell. I slide into the corner of the cot and pull my legs up to my chest.

A few hours pass and the same detective comes to the door of the cell.

"Let's go Ms. Walker."

"Where?"

He doesn't say anything but beckons for me to follow him. We walk towards the interrogation area but instead of going through the door, he takes me to the elevators.

"Have a great night." He says handing me my car keys.

"Wait, how am I supposed to get back to my car?"

"Figure it out." He says walking off.

When I get downstairs, I walk out the door without a jacket, phone or anything.

"Jayme."

I look up to see Wanda.

"Oh my God. I've never been so happy to see you. How long have you been here?"

"For over an hour. I've been trying to get information but there is nothing in the system. I was just about to leave when I saw you walking this way."

I hug her again. "How is Jace?"

"He's fine and with my babysitter. Come on, let's get out of here."

I follow her to her car.

"Are you alright?" She asks once she pulls off.

"No." I say laying my head on the seat.

"What happened?"

"They were trying to scare me."

"Who, the police?"

"No, my stepdad."

"Is he a police officer?"

"Worst, he's a pastor."

She looks at me.

"Do you know the worst part of it? No one ever believes he is this bad person capable of doing anything wrong. He's a pillar of this community, they say. He cares about the affairs of the city, they say. So I guess that means he can't be the monster I grew up with."

"What did he do to you?"

"I can probably list what he hasn't done faster."

She sighs. "I was going to talk to you today, before all of this happened, because I overhead Jace telling Josiah that his granddad is his dad."

I close my eyes at her statement.

"Is it true?"

I nod my head, yes.

"Oh honey." She says reaching over to grab my hand.

"I never wanted Jace to know. How am I supposed to explain this to him without telling him the horrors of being sexually abused by my step father?"

"I don't know sweetie but you need to try. Has your step father always been in Jace's life?"

"Not really. I left his house after finding out I was pregnant. Through the years, he'd show up, out the blue so I had to tell Jace who he was. Granddad was easier than child molester. Anyway, I hadn't seen him in a couple years but a few weeks ago, he showed up and this time he came back with a vengeance."

"What changed?"

"My mom is dying."

"Oh Jayme, I am so sorry you have to deal with all of this. What are you going to do?"

"I'm tired Wanda. Tired of being afraid and damn sure tired of running. All I can do now is fight back. For me and for Jace."

"You know I am here for the both of you, no matter what it is."

"Thank you. I don't know what I would do without you."

Chapter 12

Wanda drops me off at my car. She is going to keep Jace and send him to school tomorrow. When I get inside, I lock the doors and sitting there for a minutes before I pull off.

I stop by the hotel and pack up the things we have there before going home. I meant what I said, I am tired of running.

I get home and lock up before I pour a glass of wine and head to my bedroom. I sit the glass on the nightstand before kneeling beside the bed and saying my prayers.

It's been two weeks and things are finally starting to feel back to normal. I am back at work and Jace is back in school in enough time to make up what he has missed before Fall Break.

The next day, I am sitting in this small and cold room, nervously awaiting the doctor.

"Ms. Walker, I'm Dr. Meade. What brings you in today?"

"I'm here to be tested for HIV?"

"Have you been exposed recently?"

"Yes."

"Do you know who it was that exposed you?"

"Unfortunately, I do." I say looking at the ground.

"Did you know their status before engaging in intercourse?"

"No."

"Were you raped?"

"Can I just give some blood without all the questions?"

"Jayme, I am not trying to pry into your personal life but as your doctor, I have to ask these questions, for your safety. You know that, right?"

"Yes and I'm sorry. I don't mean to be rude but the possibility of this test being positive is pushing me further over the edge and I don't know how much more I can handle right now."

"I understand but if there is someone willing passing HIV around, you have a duty to report it."

I nod.

She taps on the IPad she's holding. "Since this is your first time here, I would you like to get a full physical on you. This way, we can test for everything, just to be on the safe side. Is that okay with you?"

I nod yes.

"Okay, here is a gown. Get completely undressed and I'll be back in a few minutes with a nurse."

I undress and sit on the table; uncomfortable, nervous and angry.

After spending an hour at the doctor's office getting pricked and prodded, I finally leave in enough time to stop by the travel agency to pick up everything Jace and I will need for our trip next week.

A few days later, Jace is sitting in the floor looking sad while flipping through the brochures.

"Jace, what's wrong?"

"Mom, it'll be okay if we can't go to Disney World this year."

"Why would you say that?"

He humps his shoulders.

"Jace listen, I know things have been crazy lately but I wouldn't let anything spoil our trip. We both need the time away."

"We're still going?"

"Of course we are."

"YES!" He screams.

He gets up and runs into his room. I pick up the brochures and smile. It is the one constant thing we've done for the past three years. Our annual trip is what I save all year for because it takes me away from the chaos of life.

While he's in his room, I sit on the couch replaying the last few days. My mom died two days ago and James has been calling, leaving messages and sending texts, trying to convince me to come to the funeral but I'll pass.

My phone vibrates, from an unknown number so I ignore it. When it stops, the same number calls again.

"Yea." I answer.

"Is this Jayme Walker?"

"Yes it is, may I ask whose calling?"

"Ms. Walker, my name is Harold Mcloughlin and I am, well I was your mother's lawyer."

"What can I do for you Mr. Mcloughlin?"

"Ms. Walker, is there a way you can meet with me?"

"Look Mr. Mcloughlin, whatever it is you have to say, please say it."

"Your mother left an insurance policy with you as the sole beneficiary along with a letter she asked me to hand deliver."

"Is this a joke?"

"I can assure you it's not. I was informed of her passing on yesterday and one of her stipulations was that I contact you as soon as possible. Can you to stop in and sign for the items? I'll be here until seven tonight."

"Sure, what's the address?"

He gives me the address and I hang up the phone.

Before I can move from the couch, my phone rings again. Maybe this time it'll be Publisher's Clearing House.

"Hello."

"Is this Jayme Walker?"

"Yes, this is she." I sigh.

"This is Regina from the office of Dr. Meade. She has the results of your bloodwork and she wants you to come in? Can you be here in an hour?"

"Sure."

"Great, see you then."

I drop Jace off at Wanda's house before stopping by the law office to sign for whatever documents Josephine left me. Getting to the car,

I throw the envelope in my purse and head to the doctor's office. By the time I am shown to Dr. Meade's office, my stomach is in knots.

"Ms. Walker, thank you for coming in on such short notice." Dr. Meade says. "I have the results of your bloodwork."

"That quick?"

"Yes, I put a rush on it because, well it looked like you were in a hurry to find out."

"Okay, I'm ready."

"Dr. Meade, there's an emergency in room one." The nurse interrupts.

"I'm so sorry, give me a second."

"Are you freaking kidding me?" I yell under my breath after she leaves.

Chapter 13

It seems as if the minutes are ticking by so slow until I hear the door open.

"Please accept my--"

"Dr. Meade, I don't mean any harm but can you just give me the results, please!"

She unlocks her IPad and turns it around for me to see.

"What am I looking at?"

"Your test results, they are all negative."

I don't say anything before picking up the IPad.

"Did you hear me?"

"Are you sure?" I stutter. "Please tell me you're sure. Even the HIV test?"

"Jayme, you do not have HIV. I recommend getting tested again every six months for the next year just to be on the safe side."

I start to cry.

"I hope those are tears of joy."

"Joy, release, confusion, hurt, pain; you name it."

"Well, it seems God has a plan for your life young lady."

I just look at her while wiping my tears. "I try to tell myself that but it's just so hard to believe I have to go through this kind of thing to grasp God's plan for my life"

"Sometimes the things we go through are not so we suffer but so that we are saved."

"Yea, well everything I've been through sure does feel like suffering to me."

"Has it not saved and strengthened you too?" She asks.

"Dr. Meade, I don't mean to sound like someone who doesn't believe in God, I do however, I have a hard time understanding why God would allow me to suffer through being molested just for Him to save me. There has to be a better way."

"Jayme, I don't know all you've been through neither do I have the absolute reasoning behind why God allows a lot of things to happen yet I know for certain that although we have God, evil also exists. Some people are just plain evil."

"I am well aware of that but why did I have to be given to two of the most evil people I know?"

"I wish I could answer that but God says in Isaiah 61:3 He will replace our spirit of despair with a garment of praise.

Dr. Meade comes from behind her desk and grabs my hands.

"I am so tired of crying."

"Then stop." She says. "Jayme, you don't have to be convinced of God's ability to heal, deliver and block what is not meant for us because your test results prove it. Yes, life is hard. Yes, things happen that break us. Yes, we have to go through hell sometimes but look at you. You are a survivor and you have a story to tell. And when you are ready to stop crying and trust God, He will give you the courage and strength to tell it."

"I don't know how to stop."

"By getting up in the morning and thanking Him. By putting one foot in front of the other and looking ahead. By believing God to do whatever it is you've been praying for and knowing He will. You are a clay pot that happens to have a few chips and dents but God is the potter who specializes in restoring what man has broken. All you have to do is put the broken pieces of your life in His hands." She stands up and pulls me into a hug. "When you do what you can, God will do what you can't. I know because I've tried Him."

I stay there for a second before pulling away.

"Thank you." I tell her,

"You are welcome. Oh, if you're interested, I run a small support group for women every second and fourth Thursday at our church, House of Hope. I'd love for you to come."

"House of Hope? Lady Stewart's church?"

"Yes, have you been there?"

"No but I met her, not so long ago, and she invited me."

"We would love to have you."

"I don't know Dr. Meade. I haven't been to church in a long time."

"Before you say no, attend one meeting and if you don't like it, you don't have to come back."

"Ok. I'll think about it."

"Great. Here's a flyer. Our next one is this Thursday."

"My son and I will be out of town but I will definitely try to make the next one. Thank you again Dr. Meade."

When I make it home, I sit on the couch in the living room, still trying to wrap my head around the test results and what Dr. Meade said.

Wanda called to say she and the boys were at the movies and she would drop Jace off afterwards so I decide to have a little praise party by myself.

I get up and pour a glass of wine before turning on some music.

After dancing around for over an hour, the doorbell rings.

Looking out the window I see a car I don't recognize. I turn the music down.

"Who is it?"

"Jacob Wallace."

I open the door.

"I apologize for dropping by unannounced." He says.

"You seem to do a lot of that. You may as well come in." I take a step back.

"Did I interrupt you?"

"No, it's fine." I say turning the music off. "What can I do for you?"

We look at each other for a few seconds and when he doesn't speak, I do.

"Is there something wrong?"

"There's something about you that is making it hard to get you off my mind."

"Look, I don't know what you think this is or who you think I am but I can assure you, it's not that type of party."

"No, please hear me out. I promise I will say this and then I'll leave."

"You have five minutes." I say taking my seat with him sitting across from me.

He sits and nervously wipes his hands on his pants.

"This is going to sound weird but from the first time I saw you, I felt a connection to you."

"Yes, this definitely sounds weird. We don't know each other so how can you possibly feel anything towards me?"

"Do you believe in spiritual connections?"

"No."

"Do you believe in God?"

"Sir, what are you getting at? Are you here because you feel sorry for me because I am nobody's charity case?"

"No, it is nothing like that, I promise you. It's weird yes but I cannot adequately explain it without making it sound weirder."

"You need to try because I find it hard to believe you right now. "Trust me, this has been even harder for me to believe but I cannot help what I feel."

"What exactly do you feel Mr. Wallace? Do you feel all the pain and hurt I've experienced over my life? Do you feel all the scars that have damaged my heart? Do you feel the anger that tries to consume me or how about the fire of rage that threatens to escape from within me? What do you feel Mr. Wallace?"

"I feel the need to save you?"

Chapter 14

"Save me?" I laugh.

"I don't mean it the way it sounds."

"Well, I heard what you said and while that is quite noble of you, I don't need saving. Where were you when I was 14 and being sexually molested by my stepdad? Or 17, when I was having my third abortion or 18 when my forth, maybe fifth suicide attempt didn't work? Or 19, when I was giving birth to my son who happens to be by this same stepdad? Where were you then because that's when I needed saving?"

He doesn't say anything.

"No words?"

"Jayme, I am not here to upset you."

"I'm not upset but I don't need smoke blown in my face either. Mr. Wallace--"

"Please call me Jacob."

"Jacob, you don't know me and if you did, I am willing to bet, you wouldn't find me worthy of being saved."

"Can I start over?"

I nod.

"Saved is not the word I should have used. God didn't send me here to save you, He did so in order for me to show you just how worthy you are to Him but you will have to let me in."

"Let you in? Did you not here what I said?"

"I heard every word."

"Then how easy do you think is for me to let anyone in, especially a man, when all I've experienced is hurt and pain? I am a broken mess Jacob. One you may want to stay clear of."

"Broken pieces can be mended." He says sitting up and clasping his hands together.

"Did you not just hear what I said?" I ask getting angry. "I am damaged and have been for a long time. There is no mending for me, I've tried! Yet every time I end right back up in the same place, looking the same demon in the face. The one who took my virginity, my dignity and most of my sanity. So you see, there is no way you can have a spiritual connection to me. I believe in God and I am trying to learn to pray again but--"

I stop and he takes a deep breath.

"Is there anything else before I show you out?" I ask.

"The bible says--"

"I don't want to hear what your bible says!"

"The bible says in Isaiah 54:4, "Fear not, you will no longer live in shame. Don't be afraid, there is no more disgrace for you. You will no longer remember the shame of your youth and the sorrows of widowhood."

I laugh. "Let me guess, you're also a preacher, Jehovah Witness or something?"

"No, I am just a man who loves God and who is obedient to what He tells me to do."

"That's funny because my stepdad said the same thing every time he would ram his penis into me. Whispering in my ear, this is God's will Jayme, don't fight it Jayme or my favorite, it's meant to be Jayme. So forgive me if I have a hard time believing in your God. He wasn't there when I needed him then and it seems like when I've been calling Him lately, things are only getting worse. Therefore, I'll pass. Thank you though, it was a very good effort.

"God is here, always has been."

"Where?" I ask looking around.

"He everywhere you are, covering and protecting you."

"Stop!" I yell jumping from my seat. "I tried praying to God but my pain is still hard to bear. And each time I try to move on, I begin to get angry trying to figure out how God could cover me but not create a way out. So forgive me Jacob but what you call protection, I call punishment."

"Those who sow in tears shall reap with joyful shouting. Psalm 126:5. Jayme, it may be hard for you to see God in all of this now but you will."

"Why are you doing this? What's in this for you? Are you trying to sleep with me? Is that it?"

"Jayme, do you remember the last time I was here?" He asks.

"Which time?"

"The day you passed out? I could have left and never looked back when you treated me like I had spit in your face or killed your dog but I didn't. Oh, I've tried to forget you, numerous time. Heck, I've even tried to disobey God and it hasn't worked well for me. This is why I'm here."

"Well, I ain't buying it. The last time your God sent me somewhere, it was to see my mom. You want to know what she told me."

I don't give him time to answer. "She said she didn't protect me because her mother didn't protect her. In fact, she said I was her sacrifice in order to get the life she had and that I should have sucked it up. Oh, that's not the worst part.

She also told me she was dying of AIDS. AIDS that my stepfather gave her. The same man who raped me a few weeks back so, again, you'll have to excuse me if I have a hard time believing this crap you're speaking."

"Please come and sit." He says patting the couch next to him.

"Look Jacob, I'm sorry for the way I've treated you and most importantly for throwing your kindness back in your face but–"

"Please?" He pats the couch again.

"This is crazy. You have to be crazy to still want to be here."

"Jayme, please. I don't want anything from you but to listen. Will you please just talk to me?

No matter what it is you have to say, I'm listening."

I reluctantly sit down next to him.

Sighing. "Do you know what my biggest fear is?"

He shakes his head no.

"That my son will become his father because they share the same blood and there's nothing I can do about it." The tears rush from my eyes before I have a chance to stop them. "Every time I look in his face I see him and I am afraid of what his future holds."

"You can break the curse."

"How? I am tired Jacob. Tired of crying and damn sure tired of fighting by myself. I never asked for this battle yet I keep getting put on the front line without any battle gear. I keep taking hits and it hurts. It hurts so badly."

"You have to give up."

Chapter 15

I look at him, very weirdly, might I add.

"Give up?"

"When you give up, you remove the block you've placed on God. It's like placing a Do Not Disturb sign on your hotel room door. As long as the sign is there, the housekeeper, whose job it is to clean, can't come in and do what he or she has a responsibility to do. But when you remove the sign, the housekeeper is then able to come in; remove the trash, change the dirty linens and make your room habitable again."

"What does that mean for me?"

"Jayme, God Is your housekeeper and He's standing outside your door, waiting for you to remove the sign in order for Him to clean up the mess that has been made in your life. Will you?"

"I want too."

"What's stopping you?"

"Everything?"

"I'm going to pray with you." He says.

"You don't have to do that."

He grabs my hands and closes his eyes.

"Our Father, it is your servant petitioning your throne. First, I want to tell you thank you. Thank you for being the creator and sustainer of life for and her son. God, you know all she's had to endure, you've seen her dark days and I know you've even felt her pain yet I thank you for keeping her. We don't know what you have planned for her life but God, I ask you to open her eyes so when she seeks you, she'll see you. God, remove the shields from her ears so she hears you when you speak.

Father, I don't want you to restore what years of abuse have taken but I want you to create new things, open new doors and shut everything that is not meant. Protect her, her son, her home and her mind. Mend what's broken, heal what is hurt and refill her joy. Answer her when she calls because she has need of you. And God, use me in the capacity in which you've sent because I trust your plan. In your son Jesus name. Amen."

When he opens his eyes, I am looking directly at him with tears streaming down my face. He slides towards me, pulling me into him and for the first time, I don't push him away. Instead, I cry and he allows me too.

"You will make it."

— — —

I open my eyes.

"Hey." He says smiling at me.

"Oh my God, did I fall asleep?"

"Yeah and I hate to tell you but you snore."

"I do not."

He laughs before removing his phone from his pocket.

"I'm sorry, I have to go." He says removing his arm from around me. "Thank you for not pushing me away, this time."

"You're thanking me? After the way I treated you, I should be the one thanking you. No matter how weird this was, it has helped in more ways than I can explain."

We both stand.

"Can I hug you?" He asks.

"Please."

He wraps his arms around me. "You're going to be alright."

"I sure hope so." I reply, releasing him.

He walks towards the door but stops. "Will it be okay if I check in on you and your son from time to time?"

"I'd like that."

"Do you still have my card?"

"Yes."

"Don't hesitate to use it, for anything. All you have to do is call."

"Wait, there is something you can do for me. Jace and I are going to Disney World next week for Fall Break. Do you mind keeping an eye out on my place?"

"Of course."

"Thanks, I'll text you my number."

"That'll be great."

I open the door and Wanda was getting ready to knock.

"Mr. Jacob!" Jace excitedly runs up to him.

"Wanda, this is Jacob. Jacob this is my friend Wanda."

They shake hands.

"I'm sorry we're late getting back. The boys wanted pizza." Wanda says.

"Oh, it's no problem. Thank you for taking care of him."

"No thanks needed. Jacob it was nice meeting you. Jayme, I'll see you later."

Jacob says his goodbyes to Jace. When I close and lock the door, I linger there a few moments with my eyes closed.

"Mom, you okay?"

"Yes baby, I am good. Go on and take your bath so you can tell me about the movie."

When he leaves, I walk into my bedroom and kneel next to my bed.

"Dear God, I am removing the do not disturb sign and I am asking you to clean up the mess I'm in. Throw away whatever it is not meant and replace it with what is. And thank you for sending Jacob. I don't know what you're doing but I'll trust you. Amen."

Chapter 16

TWO WEEKS LATER

Jace and I have been back from our trip to Disney Land for a few days now. While he's at Wanda's working on a project with her son, I decide to look for him a Halloween costume. I go to get my computer from the table and find the envelope I got from Josephine's lawyer.

With everything happening, I'd forgotten all about it. I leave the computer on the table and tear it open.

"Jay,

If you are reading this letter, I must be dead. You're probably happy about it and I don't blame you because I'm happy to finally be out this hell hole of a life. Wait, I don't know if I should be happy because I'm sure God isn't waiting on me at the gate. Anyway, after you left that day, I had time to think and you were right. I should have protected you. I am sorry. I had no right to ever put you through what I'd gone through and I hope you can forgive me. I know this doesn't take away everything you've gone through but I hope it makes life a little better.

Oh, please don't hold hate in your heart for the things that have happened. Jay, you have a chance to write a new chapter, do it. Don't try to erase the past, I've tried and it cannot be done. I didn't leave you this policy as a payoff but I left it as a way to start a new life for you and your son. I hope you will put it to good use and finally get free of James. Good luck to you and your boy.

P.S. Don't turn out like me.

Josephine."

I pull out the check and my mouth drops. $75,000.00.

"Oh my God!" I yell. "You finally got something right Josephine."

I begin dancing around the living room knowing I can now make a better life for me and Jace.

"Thank you sweet Jesus!"

I fall onto the couch, out of breath. When I finally get myself together, I go to grab my computer again but this time I see the flyer for Dr. Meade's support group.

"Dang Jayme, you need to get your memory checked."

I stand there, looking at the flyer, trying to come up with an excuse as to why I can't go but I was coming up empty. Plus I promised Dr. Meade I would, at least, try it and Jace wasn't here so I didn't have to find a baby sitter.

An hour later, I am walking through the doors of House of Hope, nervous and shaking.

The seats were in a U shape so it wasn't easy to hide so I choose a place, near the middle just as the meeting begins.

"Welcome everybody. I see some new faces in the room tonight so let me introduce myself and tell you a little about what we do here. My name is Dr. Meredith Meade and I, along with Lady Mia Stewart, are the founders of The Diary Room."

I smile when I see Officer Stewart looking at me.

"I know we are in a church building but tonight and at every meeting, we turn this room into our fortress. Inside of here, you are safe and there is no subject off limits. All we ask is for to you respect the sanctity of the diary room as well as the opinions of others."

Officer Stewart speaks. "We operate on a foundation of confidentiality so what happens in this room, stays in this room. The only way I or Dr. Meade will ever share anything is if we feel it is absolutely necessary for your safety."

"So, this is just another support group?" Someone asks.

"While we offer support, the Diary Room was created as a place to have open and honest dialogue without the fear of being judged. Understand, we don't have all the answers nor are we saying you will be completely healed but our hope is for each of you to begin walking the road to freedom." Dr. Meade says.

"Are there any more questions or concerns before we get started?" Mia asks.

We all look around but no one says anything.

"Since there are no questions, I'll ask everyone to introduce yourself and tell us whatever it is you'd like us to know about you and what you hope to get out of our meeting tonight." Dr. Meade adds.

I sit and listen to each woman, as she introduces herself and I am shocked to see such a diverse group of women who are all dealing with issues, just as I am. Some are patients of Dr. Meade while others are either members of the church or community.

The young lady next to me, taps me on the knee. I realize it's my turn and I freeze.

"It's ok, you're safe here. Take your time." Dr. Meade says.

I slowly stand and swallow the lump in my throat. "My name is Jayme and I almost didn't come tonight because fear tried to talk me into staying home. I guess, I am like a lot of you, damaged and afraid to say it out loud. Not because it will make it real, I have lived it so I know it is but more so afraid of being judged. For so long I blamed the church because the person who abused me, did so under the disguise of it being "God's will," but I know now that it wasn't the church, it was the man in the church. So after years of sexual abuse, I don't really know who I am but I am tired and I want, no I need to be free. I am not sure if this group can help me but I'm here, hoping you can."

Chapter 17

"Jayme, I am so happy you to see you."

"Officer Stewart." I say embracing her after the meeting. "How are you?"

"I am good, how are you?"

"I am doing much better. This meeting is awesome and I am glad I came. "

"So am I. Do you mind if I ask you something?"

"Sure."

We go over to an area away from everybody else.

"Is Bishop Madison your biological father?"

"God no, he's my stepdad. Why do you ask?"

"That day, on the side of the road, he was furious when you pulled off. He kept asking what you'd said to me."

"I know."

"You know? Did he hurt you?"

"Everything he does to me hurts."

"Jayme, you don't have to answer this but–_"

"Lady Mia, please don't take this the wrong way but I am not comfortable speaking to you about him."

"I understand but do you mind if I ask why?"

"Because of his connections in this city."

"You have to know that I am not connected to him, right?"

"How am I supposed to believe that?" I ask her.

"You aren't the only one he's hurt."

I don't say anything.

"You don't seem surprised." She says.

"He's a monster so I know the taste for young girls didn't stop when I left. My question to you, why are you asking me these questions now? What happened?"

She doesn't say anything.

"He hurt somebody else, didn't he?"

"Unfortunately yes. A teenage girl from a new family in the area."

"Why is he not in jail?"

"That's hard to do when he pays his victims to be quiet."

"Lady Mia, I find it hard to believe a real mother will choose money over her daughter."

He's smart so his victims are young ladies from underprivileged or broken homes. He plays on their emotions and their even stronger desire of going to college. He promises them the world and they take it. When they do, they leave and never return."

"Wow."

"This is why we need your help."

"Me? What do you think I can do? I'm 27 years old now."

"The statute of limitation has expired for you but there was a rumor, a few years back–"

"What rumor?"

"About your son."

"No, I will not bring my son into this."

"But we need your help."

"What if I had proof that he raped me recently?"

"Oh Jayme."

"No don't do that. I don't need the pity, just lock him up."

"I will do everything I can."

We spend the next thirty minutes discussing some things. By the time I stop to get Jace, from Wanda's, he's asleep. Pulling up at home, I get out to wake him when I see Jacob parked out front. I unlock the door and turn on the light inside.

"Jace, go on in. I'm right behind you."

I walk over to Jacob's car and he's asleep. Tapping on the window, I cause him to jump.

"Hey," I say when he opens the door. "How long have you been sitting here."

"About 30 minutes. Hey," he says smiling.

"You want to come in?"

"If it is not too late. I don't want to bother you."

"You're not bothering me. Come in."

He follows me inside.

"Can you lock the door while I check on Jace?"

I walk into Jace's room to find him stretched out on the bed. I get him undressed, with the promise of him getting up early to shower before school. I turn off the lights and close his door.

"Am I keeping you from getting him in bed?"

"No, he's been at Wanda's so he's worn out. Anyway, what are you doing here?"

"I was on my way home and decided to stop by to make sure you and Jace were good. I haven't seen you since your trip. You weren't here so I decided to wait a few minutes and I guess I fell asleep."

"You guess?" I laugh. "No, you did fall asleep."

His face turns red.

"I didn't mean to embarrass you. I'm glad you decided to wait. Make yourself comfortable and if you want anything to drink, help yourself, I'll be right back."

I head into my room and change into some sweats and a tank. Walking back into the living room, Jacob has his head laid back on the couch.

I grab two bottles of water from the refrigerator. Crossing over him to sit on the couch, I bump his leg.

"How are you going to make it home?" I ask when he opens his eyes.

"I'm sorry. I pulled a double today and I am worn out."

"I see."

He smiles and I hand him the water.

"How was your trip?" He asks sitting up

"It was amazing. Jace and I have been going to Disney World since he was five and we always enjoy it."

Jacob is staring at me.

"Why are you looking at me like that?"

"You seem different."

"I do?"

"Yes but in a good way. The last time I was here it seemed you had the world on your shoulders but this time, it's different, you are different."

"I guess you're right because things are different for sure."

"How so? If you don't mind me asking."

"It is kind of hard to explain but–"

Before I can say anything else, he kisses me. At first I melt into him but then I push back.

"I can't do this." I say standing up. "I'm sorry, maybe you should go."

Chapter 18

"No, I'm sorry, I shouldn't have done that. Please forgive me."

"Jacob look, I don't know what is happening but I cannot do this. Things are happening too fast and honestly, I don't know how to feel about it because I've never been with another man."

"You don't have to explain. I had no right to kiss you."

"It's just, I don't know what it means to be affectionate, to be kissed passionately, to have someone hug me without a motive or to do things for me without it costing me something in return. All I know is hurt and pain so I'm not sure I even know how it feels too genuine like anyone besides Jace because he's been the only constant thing in my life who has not hurt or let me down. "

"Jayme, I am not here to hurt you, you know that right?"

"No, I don't know that. As much as I want to believe it, I don't know how. I've never seen a relationship built on love. I've never experienced a happy home. I've never had someone keep a promise so, please forgive me but I don't know. If I can be truthful with you, I don't even understand why you're still here instead of running in the opposite direction."

"I've never been a runner."

I look at him and he laughs.

"I'm sorry, just trying to make you laugh. Look Jayme, I am not going anywhere neither will I force you to do anything that makes you uncomfortable. No matter how many times you push me away, I'll come back. You can block my calls, I'll keep calling. You can turn me away and I'll still be here for you and your son. All you have to do is let me."

I get up and start pacing the floor. "I cannot ask you to put your life on hold while I get myself together. That's not fair to you or your future. What if I am not the one and you miss out on your wife waiting around on me?"

"What if you are my wife?" He asks stopping me in my tracks.

I laugh. "Did you not hear anything I said?"

"I heard all of what you said. Did you not hear anything I just said?"

"Jacob, I don't know how to date."

"You'll learn."

"I don't know how to be in a relationship."

"We will figure it out."

"Why me though?"

"Because God sent me to pull you out of that place you think you will die in. That's why."

"What did you say?"

"Come here," he says holding out his hand that I willingly take.

"Jayme, it wasn't a coincidence you showed up at my gym that day. I wasn't even supposed to be there. Everything that has happened led me to you. It may be hard for you to believe or understand but I trust God and I know He'll never lead me somewhere He hasn't already ordained as part of my destiny. This is all God's doing and you want to know why?"

"Yes."

"Because of your inability to see him. You blame Him and the church so it's hard for you to trust Him even though you've been trying. And it's even harder for you to believe in Him even though you've been praying."

"So is this like some sort of life coaching and when you get me to a place of believing and trusting God, you'll move to your next case?"

"I'm not going anywhere girl! You are part of my destiny Jayme Walker."

I look at him.

"Yes, you heard me right and I will continue to tell you this until you believe it. I know it sounds crazy but the bible says God knows us before we are formed. To me that means, He already has our destiny planned, including who our spouses are. Sure, we make mistakes and even detour a few times but by God's mighty power and our ability to trust Him,

He will get us back on the right track that carries us to our destiny."

"I, uh, I don't know what to say in response to that."

"Say you will trust God."

"I'm trying but it's hard when I do not know everything about Him the way I should. What I do know is, I don't want to be hurt again and I'd never want to hurt someone the way I have been."

"I wouldn't do that to you."

"What if I hurt you?"

"I'm a big man."

"What if I'm afraid?"

"Will you at least try? For me?"

"I don't want to hurt you and it isn't fair for me to ask you to put up with whatever issues I'm dealing with, while I heal."

He grabs my hand, "Listen, you are not asking me to do anything, I'm here because I want to be. I cannot erase the issues of your past but I will do everything in my power to love you in your present. Neither of us know what tomorrow, the next day or even next week holds but right now I want to get to know Jayme better. That's it."

I snatch my hand from his and stand back up. "You don't understand Jacob, I come with too much baggage."

"You've already told me about your baggage and I am still here, willing to help you unpack and sort it."

"I'm just waiting for the other shoe to drop because this seems to be too good to be true." He grabs my hand again pulling me to him.

"I want you to read the book of Hosea. It's about a prostitute called Gomer. Once you're done, call me and we will talk about it. Until then, we will take it a day at a time. Is that fair?"

"Are you comparing me to a prostitute?"

"Of course not. Gomer's story is one of redemption and God used Hosea to do it. Just read it."

But--"

"Read it woman."

"Ok."

Chapter 19

I am finally back at work with a lot to catch up on. I am going through the hundreds of emails I have cyphering through the ones that have already been taken care of. If this isn't enough, I also have a new team of employees coming out of training. It's hectic. On top of that, I am trying to finish an application for this house I'm hoping I can get approved for that is in a good school zone and a gated community.

With the check from Josephine's lawyer finally clearing, I can now move forward to a new start for Jace and me.

In greater news, I haven't heard from James so all in all, things are looking up.

There is a knock on my door.

"Come in."

"Welcome back heifer." Josh says coming in causing me to laugh. "Okay then, Ms. Thang."

"What Josh?"

"I'm just saying, somebody is glowing. Spill it." He says.

I laugh. "There is nothing to spill."

"You're a bad liar. What is all this?" He says making circles in front of my face. "You look happy."

"I am."

"Who is he?"

"Why do you always think it has something to do with a man?"

"It normally is."

"Boy bye. How are things with you?"

"Ah, I'm living which is good. Jackson and I are still dating, I think."

"What do you mean, you think?"

"He hasn't been the same since his mom died. Wait, was his mom, your mom too?"

"Unfortunately."

"Girl, I am so sorry. I didn't even call you."

"It's cool. We weren't close."

"Is that why you didn't come to the funeral?"

"Yea, among other things. It's complicated and I don't want to talk about it."

"Well Jackson has been acting weird. He won't talk and I barely see him. Can you talk to him?"

"I am not doing that."

"Come on J, do it for me. Please."

"No Josh, now drop it!"

"Dang girl, I didn't mean to upset you."

"Josh, I apologize for yelling but whatever is going on with you and Jackson is between the two of you. I don't want any parts of it. Okay?"

"You're right and I shouldn't have asked. I'm sorry." He says getting up to leave. "Anyway,

I'll get out of your hair but let me know what you're doing for lunch."

When he leaves, I go out onto the floor just at the new employees are being brought from the training room.

"Hello everyone, my name is Jayme and I welcome you to First Source. I hope your weeks of training have been well spent. For the rest of today, you will be taking live calls from customers. There are two leads, Josh and Gavan, who will help with any questions. Don't try to overdo it, take your time and learn the process but I want each of you to treat every customer as you would want to be treated. Your calls are being monitored but it's only to give you critical feedback on making you effective customer service representatives. With that, I'll leave you in the hands of your leads and I'll be back to check on you."

I go back into my office just as my cell phone is ringing. I press the speaker while closing the door.

"This is Jayme."

"Hey Jayme, this is Mia Stewart. Did I catch you at a bad time?"

"No, is everything okay?"

"Yes, everything is great actually. I just left a meeting with the district attorney."

"Really? Please tell me she's going to prosecute?"

"I don't want to jinx it but they are finalizing everything needed to present James' case to a grand jury."

"Wait, I thought you needed more evidence. What changed?"

"With the statement you gave, the shirt with his DNA on it and some new evidence, we now have a stronger case."

"New evidence? From who?"

"Your brother."

"Jackson?"

"Jayme, he's HIV positive and he isn't the only one."

My mouth falls open but nothing comes out.

"Jayme, are you still there?"

"Oh my God. I found out a few weeks ago that James was HIV positive but I didn't know he'd given it to Jackson. He said James was no longer hurting him."

"Have you been tested?"

"Yes and thank God, I am negative but are you saying he has infected more people?"

"At least five that we know of."

"That no good, low down dirty dog."

"That's not the worst of it because some of the victims aren't even eighteen."

"No Mia, please don't tell me--" I stop when my voice cracks. "He has ruined their lives."

"Yes and it's sad it had to come to this but others are willing to stand up against him now. We got him Jayme. We finally got him!"

"Let's pray it sticks because he doesn't deserve the chance to hurt anybody else. Thank you, so much, for all your help. If it hadn't been for you pressing the issue, we wouldn't be here."

"No, thank you for being willing to testify. I will be in touch with the court date."

When I hang up, I do a dance in the office before texting Jacob with the great news.

Chapter 20

The following Saturday afternoon, Jace and I are with Jacob. He will not tell us where we're going, only to say there is somebody he wants us to meet.

During the entire car ride, he doesn't say anything. He pulls up to a house in a beautiful subdivision of Olive Branch.

"Whose house is this?"

He ignores me and instead turns the car off, gets out and opens my door.

"Please tell me we are not about to meet your parents?"

"I won't."

"No Jacob, I am not ready."

He grabs my hand pulling me from the car. "You'll be fine, come on."

He opens the door for Jace and we follow him up the steps. He unlocks the door, walking in.

"Mom, dad?"

A gorgeous middle age woman comes around the corner with a huge smile on her face.

"Jacob? What do we owe this surprise?" She asks hugging him.

"Mom, I want you to meet Jayme and Jace."

"Finally." She says pulling me into a hug. "It's so nice to meet you. I am Diane and this is my husband Michael. Jacob has told us so much about you."

I look at Jacob.

"You don't have to be shy because I feel like I already know you." She says. "And you must be Jace?"

"Yes ma'am." He says as I shake Michael's hand.

"Well come on in." She leads us to the living room.

"Jacob, why don't you and your dad show Jace around while Jayme and I talk."

We head into the kitchen where she is cooking.

"It smells great in here."

"Thank you. I'm making pasta for lunch. I hope you and Jace will eat with us." She says walking over to stir something in one of the pots before replacing the top and turning around.

"Have a seat because I want to talk to you alone for a minute."

"Okay."

She turns off the pot and comes over to the bar. "Jayme, I hope you don't mind but Jacob told us some of the things you've been through."

"I see. Is this going to be one of those, leave my son alone because you're no good for him, type of conversation?"

"No dear, in fact, it is just the opposite."

"What do you mean?"

"Ever since Jacob met you, you're all he talks about. It's crazy because he has never talked about anybody else as much as he talks about you."

"And you're okay with him dating somebody like me?"

"Somebody like you? What does that mean?" She asks looking confused.

"Well, you said he has told you what I've been through so I assume you know about the sexual abuse?"

"I do."

"And you're okay with it knowing there is a big possibility of me hurting him?"

"Yes."

"Why?"

"Because I've been to the place you're trying to get free from. I was molested by my grandfather."

I sit up straighter and look at her.

"Is this a joke?"

"Baby, I would never joke about anything like this because there is nothing funny about it. Trust me, I know how hard it is to walk in those shoes. And just like you, I received the one of my biggest blessings, Jacob."

She continues to speak. "I was eleven when Poppa, as he liked to be called, began assaulting me. At first it was simple gestures everyone thought were cute. You know, little kisses on the cheek, holding my hand, sitting me in his lap and things like that. It wasn't until I started staying with him that things got worse."

"Why did you have to live with him?"

"My mother was on drugs and to keep me from going into foster care, I was sent to stay with my grandparents. Everybody said it was the best thing for me but nobody told me the real reason my mom was strung out on drug."

"He did the same thing to her?"

"Yes and she did nothing to stop it from happening to me. On my thirteenth birthday, he, according to his words, made me a woman."

She stops and takes a deep breath before continuing. "That night would be the first time he forced himself on me but it surely wouldn't be the last."

"Did you tell anyone?"

"Oh yes. I told my grandmother and she beat the hell out of me. Afterwards, she pulled me from school and told me if I ever told anybody, my grandfather would kill me."

"What made it stop?"

"It was either the third or fourth time, I got pregnant. I couldn't take any more of the methods my grandmother would use to make me lose the baby, so I ran. I was almost eighteen so I worked a few odd jobs to save up for a train ticket to Memphis. When I got here, I was homeless for a few weeks before I started working as a housekeeper in a hotel downtown. The manager let me stay in one of the rooms until I could get on my feet. I had Jacob and a year later, I met Michael. They were my saving grace."

"Is that why Jacob likes me because I remind him of you?"

"God no, my son likes you for you."

"How can you be sure because all of this seems crazy and truthfully, I am waiting for the other shoe to drop?"

"What do you mean?"

"I am waiting for Jacob to wake up and realize he has made a mistake being with someone like me."

"Jayme, I know my son and he really likes you. His eyes light up when he talks about you, even before he knew your story."

"But I am damaged and I don't know if I can give him what he is giving me."

"You will eventually. Look Jayme, I know how scared you are to let someone in but if you never try, how will you know what you're capable of?"

"How long was it for you?"

"Baby, some days are still hard but in the beginning of our relationship, it took me and Michael over a year to be intimate but he was patient. There were days I couldn't even look into Jacob's face because he reminded me of all the hell I'd gone through but then he would smile at me and with every smile, it repaired a piece of my broken heart."

"When did you tell Jacob everything?"

"When he was old enough to understand. I didn't want to hide it from him because I couldn't allow the pattern of abuse to continue. So I told him to break the generational curse."

"Wow." I say getting up and walking to the back door. "I don't know how to respond Mrs. Diane because I told Jacob the same thing about Jace."

"Jace doesn't have to turn out like the man who did these things to you and the only person who can stop it is you."

"How?"

"You'll have to let someone else in. If not, you run the risk of never getting rid of the voices and the nightmares."

"All of my life I've never had anyone to look at me the way Jacob does. I've never had anyone around my son and every day it is hard but I am trying because I don't want to mess up the heart your son has."

"You won't."

"How can you be sure?"

"Because his heart is in God."

Chapter 21

Walking over to me, she grabs my hands.

"Jayme, you will make some mistakes. There will even be days you're going to lash out and push Jacob away but he will be there."

"Until he's not." I say.

"I'm not going anywhere." He says coming into the kitchen.

"You say that now but one day your patience will run out. Every day I wake up thinking I am going to fail my son or that I'll make you hate me because I can't let you in. I'm trying not too but it's hard."

"Where is God Jayme?" His mom asks.

"I wish I knew."

"He's right here." She says touching my chest. "He's in your heart. You just have to trust that He'll strengthen you when you're at your lowest."

"I'm trying, I promise I am."

"Can we pray for you?" She asks as Michael and Jace walk into the kitchen.

Jace walks over and grabs my hand. They all surround me and his dad begins to pray and his mom begins speaking in a language I'd never heard of. The more they pray, the harder I cry until I am down on my knees. Jace wraps his arms around me.

"Oh God! Please help me because I am tired and cannot do it anymore." I hug Jace tighter. After a few minutes I feel hands on my back as Diane begins praying.

"Dear God, we rebuke the hand of the enemy from Jayme's life and we cover her and Jace by your blood. Today God, we speak healing and deliverance in order to break every chain of suicidal thoughts, every yoke of bondage and cast out every spirit of iniquity. God, we speak restoration and peace. We speak your protection and provision for you are a mighty God. And we believe by your power that Jayme shall be made whole. Do it for her now, oh God. And hear her plea because we trust you and we take you at your word to never leave nor forsake us. In your name we pray. Amen."

On the way home, I decide it is time for Jace and me to find a church home.

The next morning, I go into Jace's room to wake him up.

"Hey sleepy head. Get up."

"Where we going?" He asks wiping his eyes.

"To church."

"Really?"

"Yes."

He throws his comforter back and jumps out of bed. While he's in the bathroom, I lay out some clothes for him to wear before going to shower and dress.

I decide to visit House of Hope and it turns out, Wanda and Josiah are members there too.

Walking into the church, I can't tell what's shaking more, my hands or legs but the warm welcome and hugged by the greeters allows me to calm down. We are shown to our seats by an ushers. I look around to see if I can find Wanda but the sanctuary is huge so, Jace and I find sit toward the middle.

Service begins and by the time the praise teams finishes I begin to feel like I've been missing out on this. A gentleman gets up, dressed in casual clothes and it isn't until he speaks that I realize he's Mia's husband, Pastor Reymont Stewart.

"Before I take my sermon, I am feeling a heaviness in my spirit. I don't know who it is for but God says, welcome home. He says you've been running from him but He's glad you got tired."

I am looking around and although nobody is looking at me, it feels like there is a spotlight pointed directly at me.

"Beloved, whomever you are, God says welcome home, He's glad you came and He's glad you showed up because He has something for you."

Then the praise team begins to sing, "I am redeemed, bought with a price Jesus has changed my whole life. If anybody asks you just who I am, tell them, I am redeemed."

By the time the song finishes and the music is low, I am full bawling and so is most of the congregation. Even through my tears, it feels like weight is being lifted from me. I raise my hand in praise as I shout Jesus over and over.

"There she is." I hear Pastor Stewart says. "Welcome home daughter."

Wanda walks over and pulls me into the aisle, toward the altar where I fall to my knees. I can hear Pastor Stewart but I cannot see him. All I feel is something happening that I cannot explain.

I don't know how long I stay on my knees but the spirit of God was so heavy. By the time I stand up, Pastor Stewart is praying over the other men and women who were also on the altar.

I'd never seen anything like it but because the spirit had taken over, Pastor Stewart didn't even get a chance to preach.

After service, I am sitting on the front row trying to wrap my head around what happened. Wanda said I wasn't the only one set free because there were over thirty more people who came forward.

As I try to grasp what she is saying, Pastor and Lady Mia comes over.

"Pastor, this is the young lady I told you about." Mia says.

"Young lady, I am so happy you came today."

I wipe the residual tears from my face as he kneels in front of me. "God has made the way out of bondage but in order to truly be free, you have to first forgive yourself. No matter what or who hurt you before, they no longer have the power to hurt you anymore. The door is open, you just have to come out."

He stands up and extends his hand to me. When I take it, he pulls me up. "And if you need more of a reason, he's right here."

I look over at Jace who has tears falling too, standing next to Wanda. I reach out my hand and he comes to me.

"I'm ready. I'm ready to forgive and be free."

"While you are forgiving those who hurt you, forgive yourself too."

Chapter 22

We decide to do lunch with Wanda and Josiah and it gave me the chance to ask her questions, I felt too embarrassed to ask the pastor. She was patient and answered them all. She even invited me to come with her to bible study on Wednesday night.

As we're leaving Logan's Restaurant, my phone rings.

"Hey," I answer.

"Did I catch you at a bad time?" Jacob asks.

"Oh no, Jace and I are just leaving lunch with my friend Wanda."

"Well since you've already had lunch, would you and Jace like to catch a movie?"

"Sure."

"Cool. Meet me at the Malco Theater on Goodman and Airways. I'll be there in about twenty minutes."

"See you then."

Jace picks the movie Peter Rabbit and he loved it. Walking out, Jace is in front of us and for the first time I hold Jacob's hand.

"What are you doing for Thanksgiving?" He asks.

"Um, I haven't really thought about it because it's normally just me and Jace."

"Mom asked me to invite you and Jace for dinner. My brother and his wife will be there and a few of my aunts and uncles."

"I don't know Jacob. What if--"

"Just think about it. If you're not comfortable, I understand."

"No, you know what, tell her we will be there."

He smiles before walking us to my car. Before I get in, he kisses me on the lips.

"Thank you for a wonderful afternoon." I tell him.

"Thank you for accepting my invitation. Call me when you get home."

"Why don't you come home with us and we can have ice cream?"

"You sure?"

"Of course."

"See you in a bit."

When I get in the car, I look back at Jace and he's smiling.

"What are you smiling about?"

"Mom, I really like Mr. Jacob." He says putting his seatbelt on.

"Me too."

Getting home, Jace and Jacob are wrestling over the remote while I go to get the ice cream from the freezer.

"I hate to be the bearer of bad news but this ice cream is old."

"Aw man!" Jace says.

"Well how about Jace and I go and grab some while you change clothes."

"That sounds like a great idea."

Jacob kisses me again. "We'll be right back."

I stand there a few seconds touching my lips. "Is this what love feels like?" I ask into the air. "If it is, God, please let it last."

I walk into the bedroom and remove my dress and tights, putting on a long, comfortable lounge type dress. I straighten up my bedroom, while I have a little time and when I walk back up front, I stop in my tracks.

"What are you doing here?"

"Did you think I would let you testify against me? I've worked too hard for what I have and I will not allow some low life slut to take it all away. Do you know what you've done?"

"ME! What I've done? What about what you've done! You were the one who raped me. You did this, not me!"

"You ruined my life."

"And you ruined mine."

He laughs. "Good thing a dead girl is no good to the prosecution."

"You may shut my mouth but I'm not the only one who is finally bold enough to stand up against you now."

"What?"

"Oh, your high power people didn't tell you? Apparently, I wasn't the only one daddy had a taste for."

"You mean Jackson?" He laughs. "He was easier to deal with than you."

"What did you do?"

"He should have known not to bite the hand that feeds you."

"What did you do to Jackson?"

"Let us call it, tying up loose ends."

"You sick bastard!"

"Yeah, I maybe but whose going to stop me? With you and Jackson out of the way--"

"What about the others? Are you going to kill them too?"

"What others?"

"Those who you were supposed to be praying over but instead you preyed over. See daddy, I am not the only one testifying against you. So killing me won't stop the fact that it's over for Bishop James Madison. A man who was supposed to serve God but instead, you passed around HIV. Do you know how many lives you've ruined?"

"SHUT UP!" He yells. When he looks off I take a chance on getting to my phone. Before I can, he grabs me.

"James, let me go."

"You want me to let you go?" He releases my arm and before I can move, he punches me in the face.

I stumble back, falling to the floor.

"HELP!" I scream. "HELP!"

He kicks me, over and over. "I should have done this a long time ago." He says between kicks. He straddles me, punching me again. "You are nothing more than a filthy whore who doesn't know when to keep her mouth."

He punches me again. "It's a shame you'll have to die, leaving me to raise our son. Our young, fresh and ripe son. I'll be sure to take good care of him for you."

He bends down to kiss me but I spit blood into his face. "You'll never lay a finger on him again, you sick son-of-a-bitch."

He punches me again and it's the last thing I remember.

I open my eyes and begin fighting when I see a man standing over me.

"Jayme, baby calm down. You're safe."

"Where am I?"

"You're in the hospital."

I close my eyes and all of the images, of what happened, start flooding back.

"James?"

"He's in jail."

"Jace?"

"He's with my parents, in the waiting room."

"Did he see–"

"No, he didn't see anything."

"What happened? The last thing I remember is being punched."

"One of your neighbors heard your screams for help. She called the police and by the time they got there, she'd knocked him out with a baseball bat. She has one hell of a swing."

"Remind me to thank her."

I feel my face. "Ah!" I touch my lip. "Why is all of this happening to me? Why is God punishing me? Just when I think my life is starting to get better, this happens. "

"God isn't punishing you. He's--"

"I don't want to hear this is part of His plan. I am tired Jacob."

"Babe, calm down." He says touching my leg.

"No! Just leave me alone Jacob. Leave me alone and get out!"

"Sir, if you can please step out until we can get her calm?"

"Nurse, you can give her whatever you need to but I am not leaving. I'll step out of the way while you do your job but I am not leaving her."

"I am damaged goods and--"

Chapter 23

My eyes flutter open and I see Jacob sitting beside my bed.

"You're still here?"

"I told you I am not leaving. You can fight me all you want but I am staying."

"You say that now but it's only a matter of time before you do." I raise my hand to wipe my mouth.

He walks over, grabs a towel and wipes my mouth before sitting on the side of the bed. I snatch it from his hand.

"I'm not leaving Jayme."

"Do you really want to put up with all this?"

"I am not putting up with anything. If this is what you have to go through to come out whole and healthy, so be it but I am not leaving."

"Why though? You can have any girl you want."

"I don't want a girl, I want a woman and that's you." He bends down to kiss me but the door opens and Jace comes running in.

"Mom, are you ok?"

I grab his hand. "You've been crying?"

"Why are you talking funny?" He asks.

"I just bit my lip, that's all. I will be okay."

"Are you coming home tonight?"

I look at Jacob who shakes his head.

"No, I have to stay here a little while longer."

"Can I stay here with you?"

"Why don't you come home with us?" Jacob's mom says.

Jace looks at me.

"Would you like that?" I ask him.

He shrugs.

"It'll be better than being cooped up in this old stinking hospital room. What do you say?"

"But I don't have any clothes or my tablet. What about school?" He whines.

"Jace,"

"Jace look," Diane says walking over to him. "I know you're scared and you barely know us but I can promise you, we will not hurt you. We will get you whatever you need for school and we will take care of you until your mom comes home."

"You will take me to school?"

"Of course." She answers.

"Okay." He says before giving me a kiss.

"Be on your best behavior and I'll see you tomorrow. Mrs. Diane, I'll call the school in the morning to give authorization to you and Mr. Michael."

Once they leave, Jacob comes back to the bed, snuggling up beside me. I moan in pain.

"I'm sorry."

"No, stay."

He gets comfortable as he can and pulls me into him.

"Please don't hurt us because my heart cannot take anymore." I tell him.

"I won't, I promise."

"I'm serious Jacob. Jace has been through more in his lifetime than any little boy should. If you cannot handle it, leave now."

He raises my head and softly kisses me to shut me up. "I am here for you and for Jace. All you have to do is give me a chance."

There is a knock on the door and a doctor walks in.

"How are you feeling?"

"Like I've been kicked around." I reply as Jacob moves.

"I'm Dr. Sambi and I'll be overseeing your care while you're with us. You have some bruised ribs, a cut on your forehead that required about four stitches, a busted lip and a small fracture of the nose. Your lip didn't require stitches but we used some glue to close up the wound. I was able to realign your nose without surgery. We wrapped your chest to help with the ribs but I will not lie, you'll be in some pain while they heal. Other than that, we will keep you overnight and if all goes well, you can go home tomorrow. Do you have any questions?"

"Can I get something for pain?"

"Sure. I'll send the nurse in with something and I'll be back in the morning."

When he leaves, Jacob walks back over.

"He said I may be able to go home tomorrow but I don't even know where that is anymore." I say wincing in pain.

"We will worry about that tomorrow."

I wake up, I'm guessing a few hours later and Jacob is gone. I don't even remember him leaving. The room is quiet and there's only a small light on. I feel the bandage on my forehead before rubbing my lip and running my hand across the bandage under my gown.

I sigh.

"Dear God, I am sure I've said this before but I don't know what else to say or what other words to pray so all I have left is, I surrender. Whatever you have for my life, grant it. And whatever or whoever is not meant, remove it. Amen."

———

The next morning Jacob walks in with some bags. "How are you feeling, this morning?"

"Better, how are you?"

"As long as you are good, so am I." He says giving me a kiss after dropping the bags.

I smile.

His phone vibrates and he turns it around to show me a picture of Jace from his mom. He's blowing me a kiss.

"Aw, that's too cute. Please thank your mom and dad for me. They didn't have to take care of Jace."

"They are loving it." He says. "I hope you don't mind but I went by your apartment to get you something to put on. I also got your toothbrush and a few other things. I made sure everything was locked up and here's your phone.

"You did all that and you think I mind?"

"Well, I did have to go through your things."

"Man, you know the dirty parts of my life. Seeing my closet is easy."

There is a knock on the door. Jacob opens it to Mia and the detective from the night I was falsely arrested.

"Jayme, how are you feeling this morning?"

"I'm good Mia, how are you?"

"I am good as well, his is Detective Lewis."

"I remember him." I say rolling my eyes. "This is Jacob."

"Hey Jacob, it's good to see you again." Mia says.

"Ms. Walker, let me apologize for my actions the first time we met. I had no idea the kinds of things Bishop Madison was capable of. It wasn't until you left that I begin to dig into his past. Then I was contacted by Officer Stewart."

"That's supposed to make me feel better? You put me out in the cold without a jacket or a phone."

"I know and I am very sorry."

"Why are y'all here? Please don't tell me James is out."

"Jayme," Mia cuts in. "No, we are not here about that but I do have something to tell you."

"Just tell me."

"Your brother Jackson was found dead this morning."

I close my eyes. "How did he die?"

"He was kidnapped and tortured by some low life thugs. We have them in custody and they have already confessed to James being the person who paid them to do it."

"What is wrong with that man? Please tell me there is no way he can get away with any of this."

"I can guarantee we will do everything in our power to make sure he never sees the light of day again."

"I sure hope so."

"As next of kin, you have the say on what happens to your brother's body, when it is released in a few days. I gave the medical examiner's office your contact."

"Thank you Mia, for everything."

"I am just happy you're okay and we got that piece of trash off the streets. We will get out of here and let you rest. Call me if there is anything I can do."

When they leave, I yell out, "Lord, I will be glad when my season of suffering is over."

"Our suffering never ends but it does get easier." Jacob says grabbing my hand.

"From your lips to God's ears."

"I'm going to go down to the cafeteria to get something to eat. You want anything?"

"Some coffee would be great."

"Coming right up."

He holds the door for a nurse as he's leaving out.

"Your husband really loves you." She says.

"Oh, he's not my husband."

"Not yet." She says smiling. "I'm Justine and I'll be your nurse until 7pm. How is your pain today, on a scale from one to ten?"

"About a seven."

"I'll get you something to help with that. I'll also change the bandage over your stitches." She washes her hands and puts on gloves. "So, how long you two been together?"

"A couple of months."

"Wow, by the way he looks at and protects you, I would have easily guessed years."

"I wish."

She looks at me. "No honey, you don't wish, you pray."

"I'm learning that."

"Yea, it's something I had to learn myself." She says removing the bandage from my head. "Sometimes, we can get so caught up in the bad things that happen to us in life until we miss seeing the good. But that fellow, he's a good one."

"I surely hope so."

"Isn't it funny how life can knock you down but God will be standing right there to pick you up? God will let you go through hell with one somebody as preparation for the one that will last until death due you part. Humph, I know because I've been there."

She finishes up and grabs my hand. "Okay, I have you all finished up. Oh, let me put some moisture on your lips."

She comes back with a tube and slides it on. "That'll do it. I'll get your pain medicine and be right back."

When she walks out, I laugh a little before looking up.

"I hear you God."

Chapter 24

I am finally released from the hospital, after two days but going back to my place was not an option. Jacob did not give me a chance to even bring up the idea of a hotel before offering his guest rooms to me and Jace.

Getting settled in the room across from his, Jacob comes in with the few things he'd picked up from my place.

"You didn't have to do all this. I could have gone to a hotel." I tell him, sitting the bed.

"Girl, you know that ain't happening." He says with the phoniest country accent causing me to laugh before I grab my side.

"I'm sorry, I shouldn't be making you laugh."

"No, it's just what I need." I say sitting on the bed.

"Babe, listen." He says walking over and kneeling in front of me. "I am not expecting you to move in, unless you want to." He winks. "But you definitely need to find somewhere else for you and Jace to live. That place is a part of your past and as long as you stay there, it will continue to haunt you. Starting over gives you the chance to really heal."

I smile. "I know and I actually applied for this house to rent but stuff keeps happening.

That reminds me, I need to call my boss and Josh."

"Go on, make your phone calls and I'll be back to check on you."

When he stands up, I grab his hand and slowly stand up, wrapping my arms around his neck.

"Thank you." I say before covering his mouth with mine.

Jace comes running in. "Ugh!"

I step back from Jacob and laugh at Jace who has his eyes covered.

"Boy, get over here and give me a hug. How was school?"

"It was awesome. It was Science day and we got to touch some frogs."

"Ugh, frogs?"

"Aw mom, they aren't so bad." He says hopping on the bed. "Grandma Wallace says we staying here?"

"It's we are and yes, is that alright with you?"

"Cool!" He says jumping up and down.

"It looks like someone has had a little bit of sugar." I say to him.

"Just a little." He laughs.

Jacob places his hands on Jace's shoulders to stop him. "Well Mr. Wild Man, let us allow your mom to rest while I show you where you will be sleeping."

When they leave, I grab my phone but Diane taps on the door.

"Hey sweetie, is there anything you need?"

"No ma'am, I am good. Thank you for taking care of Jace. You didn't have to."

"It has been our pleasure. Having him around has been a blessing to Michael and I but are you sure you are alright?"

I slowly sit back down. "Mrs. Diane, all of this seems too good to be true. It feels like I will wake up and find out I've been dreaming this entire time."

"What if it is?" She asks.

I look at her.

"What if it is Jayme, what would you do?"

"I don't understand."

"What if something happened tomorrow that shakes up your world again, will you still trust God? What if, let's say, something happened to Jacob, God forbid, and you find yourself starting over again, will you still trust God?"

"I don't know."

"And that's a natural response because none of us really knows what will happen, minute by minute, but for right now, we are here for you and that little boy. I don't know why God sent Jacob into your life but I am glad He did."

She walks over and hugs me.

"Dinner will be ready in a little while. Why don't you take a shower and rest and I'll send Jacob to get you when it's ready."

"Thank you." I say to her as she turns to walk out.

Before I can walk into the bathroom, my phone rings. I put it on speaker and lay it on the bed while I grab some clothes.

"Hey Wanda."

"Jayme, are you okay. I've been so worried about you then Josiah came home and said you're in the hospital."

"I was but I'm home, well I'm staying with Jacob. I was attacked."

"Oh my God Jayme. Do they know who attacked you? "Yes, it was my stepdad but he's in jail now. Girl, this has been a nightmare. I'll have to tell you about it."

"I am just thankful you're okay. Do you need me to get Jace or grab some things from your apartment?"

"No, I am good for now and Jacob's parents have been getting him back and forth to school."

"Okay but if there is anything you need, call. I don't care the day or the time."

"Thank you Wanda, I don't know what I would have done without you."

"No thanks needed. Take care of yourself."

When I hang up from her, I make the calls to my boss Evelyn and Josh. Hearing Josh cry breaks my heart. I tell him, I will keep him updated on the arrangements for Jackson.

Stripping down, I realize a shower isn't a great idea with these bandages so I have to do an old fashion wash up. I have to laugh at myself because I didn't realize how hard this would be and by the time I am done, I've broken out into a sweat.

I decide to lay down for a while.

"Did you think you could get rid of me?" I gasp at the tightness around my neck. "You'll never be free from me. You're mine!"

"No! Stop!"

"Jayme, baby, it's me. Jayme."

I open my eyes to Jacob before bursting into tears.

"You were having a bad dream."

"Will I ever be free Jacob?"

"Of course you will. God's word says in 2 Corinthians 3:17, now the Lord is the Spirit, and where the Spirit of the Lord is, there is freedom. If you stay in Him, you have no choice but to be free." He wipes the tear falling from my eyes.

"Will you lay with me a little while?"

He climbs in the bed behind me and I close my eyes. "You can rest and although I can't fight for you in your dreams, I'll do so in the spirit."

BREAKING NEWS

"Following up on the breaking news story, we bought you earlier today, Local Memphis Pastor, James Madison was arrested this morning at his home in Tipton County. According to arrest records and information we've obtained, Bishop Madison is accused of First Degree Murder, fifteen counts of Sexual Abuse of a minor, five counts of Criminal Transmission of HIV and more.

Madison is the Senior Pastor of Fellowship of Christ, where he has served for over fifteen years. He is also a Chaplain with Methodist Hospital and serves as head of the faith based initiative, Pastors against Abuse or PAA; an organization started last year to wage war against Domestic Violence and Sexual Abuse."

"I don't believe it, there is no way he could have done this. I don't buy it. Bishop Madison has been a staple in the community since I was a little girl." A witness says.

"No comment. Direct all questions to Fellowship of Christ's legal team."

"You know it is a sad day for the city when someone like Bishop Madison can be charged with such horrendous things. If he is guilty, God will deal with him." Another witness says.

"Those are just a few of the comments we've had since the arrest of Bishop James Madison. We reached out to his attorney who has declined to comment. A local crew went by the administrative offices of the church but they wouldn't speak to us either. We will bring you the latest on this developing story at 10PM on News Channel 36."

Chapter 25

It's been three weeks since everything happened. Thanksgiving has come and gone and although I have a lot to be thankful for, it was hard to be happy when I still had to plan a memorial service for Jackson.

I held a small service at Harrison Memorial Funeral home, on his birthday, November 27th and buried him next to Josephine.

I have the Madison home being placed on the market and an estate sale for all the things inside. There is nothing I want from that house.

As if dealing with lawyers and real estate folk, wasn't bad enough, now, I have to deal with all the curve balls and accusations James has been throwing out as a way to get out of going to jail.

Today, Jace is having a court ordered DNA test because James' defense team says I'm lying about him being Jace's father. Once we're done here, I am meeting with the prosecutor and her team to go over documents in preparation for trial.

One small victory was the judge denying James a bond due to the murder charge. The prosecutors are hoping to reach a plea deal to avoid putting the victims through a trial but knowing James, he'll never agree.

While we wait, I turn my phone on to multiple voicemail alerts. Before I can listen to any of them, an unknown number calls.

"Hello. Yes, no what happened? Are you freaking kidding me? Hold on." I motion for Jacob to follow me outside as I put the phone on speaker.

"Can you repeat that?"

"James Madison was killed last night."

"How?"

"He was stabbed to death by another inmate, who happens to be a father of one of the victims."

"Wait, how did they end up in the same pod?" Jacob asks.

"No one knew the identity of the other inmate until it was too late. Apparently, his last name is different from the victim's and he was already in before James was sent there."

"Wow."

"The prison officials are still investigating but as of now, there is no need for us to meet. Once I have more information I will let you know."

"Mrs. Shelton, are you sure it was James?"

"Yes ma'am. I've seen the body myself."

"And you're sure he's dead?"

"Yes ma'am."

"Then I am good. Matter of fact, I am better than good and this is all the information I need."

"Are you sure?"

"Very. You have a very good day."

I hang up the phone and look at Jacob before throwing my hands around his neck.

"I am finally free."

THREE MONTHS LATER

~Diary Room~

"Welcome, ladies, to the Diary Room. Dr. Meade had an emergency and will not be able to join us but that will not keep us from spending a little time together. Our subject for the month of March is forgiving ourselves. How many of you know it's alright to forgive yourself?" First Lady Mia asks.

I look around but I don't see a lot of hands.

"Many times we focus so much on forgiving others that we forget about forgiving ourselves. When this happens, it causes us to stay stagnant or stuck in situations that are not good for us. We become comfortable and before we realize it, we have spent years in the wrong place. Reality is, we think we can't do any better than our current circumstance so we make it up in our mind to deal with the hell, we've always dealt with because it's easier than starting over. We put up with abuse out of shame and we hide our scars because of fear. We give power to our past and it sucks the life out of our present. Well ladies, that ends tonight because we are forgiving ourselves and taking back our power."

The ladies clap and amen.

"Before we get into our discussion and activity, there is someone who is willing to share her story, in the hope it helps somebody else."

She motions for me and I walk up to the front.

"Hello ladies, my name is Jayme and I am overcoming sexual abuse. No, I didn't say I am an overcomer because I'm still trying to get over it but I'm farther along today than I was yesterday so I'm overcoming. For me, the abuse started when I was 14, by my stepdad and it almost took my life. For years I was broken, feeling like God had forsaken and forgotten about me. I was at a point in my life where I didn't mention God's name because I blamed Him for everything happening to me. I mean, why would a God who says He loves and cares about us allow us to be abused. I was angry y'all. Angry at everybody and everything. But in the midst of the hell, God sent a man. I ask God, really?"

Some of the ladies chuckle.

"Here I am dealing with sexual abuse by a man and you send another man to help me? How is that possible when the only male I halfway trust is my son? Then a woman told me and I'll never forget this. She said, God will let you go through hell with one somebody as preparation for the one that will last until death due you part. Yet, I couldn't fully let him in until I first forgave myself because when I stopped to really think, I realized the person I blamed the most wasn't God, it was me."

"Amen to that." Somebody says.

"I realized that all these years, I blamed me even though I couldn't stop it or prevent it. I used to lie awake at night thinking, maybe if I hadn't looked at him like that or maybe if I hadn't worn that skirt or those shorts or maybe if I had told somebody. I blamed myself then but not anymore because I have since learned to forgive myself. I had to forgive that 14 year old and I forgive this 27 year old because there is more years ahead of me than behind and I refuse to live them in fear and bondage. I even forgave my mom and stepdad because I realized, God's wrath was more powerful than mine."

I pause. "Forgiveness allowed me to live again. And for somebody tonight, your freedom is in your ability to forgive yourself. Don't go through another year holding on to the mistakes and the failures. Tonight, tomorrow or the day after; strive to forgive you."

"Are you able to love again?" One lady asks.

"Yes even though some days are hard, I am beginning to see and feel true genuine love. God has blessed me with a great man who adores both me and my son. He is patient with me as I fight each day but this time my fight is not against him but it's for my freedom. Some days are harder than others but I'm equipped now with the word of God and prayer."

Another lady raises her hand. "This may be going too far but is it hard to be intimate?"

"Very but intimacy, for me, isn't about sex. We have yet to go there but we have been intimate and that is those nights he pulls me into his arms and tell me he loves me, is praying for me and most importantly fighting for me. It is also those nights, when my thoughts are trying to consume me and I pull away from him and he tells me, he will be waiting when I'm ready. So, yes it is very hard, some nights but I am strong enough, now to fight it. You know why? Because I refuse to allow the torment of being a victim to hold me hostage any longer. And I be doggone if I allow fear to keep me from consummating our marriage on my wedding night."

"You go girl!" Someone yells out.

"Ladies, I am not an overnight success story because it's only been a few months since I began the forgive me process but it's worth it. Take it one day at a time and don't be afraid to let others in. Also, if you need help, ask for it."

"Are there any more questions for Jayme?" Mia asks.

There aren't any so I take my seat as Mia walks over to the side of the room and pulls this big board in front.

"This is a forgiveness board. On this board, I want you to write something you forgive yourself for. This is not a board to forgive momma, baby daddy or friend but it's to write what you are forgiving you for. Let's take thirty minutes and sign it. Afterwards, if you want to share a piece of your story with the class, you will have the opportunity to do so. She hands out markers and the ladies all spread out and begin writing.

After thirty minutes or more, we all regroup.

"Thank you ladies and I hope you enjoyed this exercise. Is there anyone who wants to share what they are forgiving themselves for?"

A few of the women give their testimonies and by the time the meeting is over, we are all a crying mess.

"Ladies, tonight we take back our healing. We are leaving this room, beginning the process to be forgiven and free and I pray that God's will shall be done in each of your life. I know there isn't a magic pill to erase everything you've gone through but I hope you leave here stronger. As always, if you need someone to talk to, call my office at the church and I will be glad to set you up with a therapist. Let us pray."

When I get home, Jacob is asleep on the couch with Jace on his chest. I take out my phone and snap a picture before sitting across from them.

I don't bother to wake them, yet, because watching them allows me to reflect back on the last six months and all the things that have happened.

One of the things that helped the most is the memory of the night Jacob told me to read about Gomer, in the bible. Although my story is different from Gomer, I could relate to feeling just as unworthy as she did. I put myself into Gomer's shoes, the many times she ran from Hosea who only wanted to help her yet she couldn't accept it because she didn't feel worthy. Gomer helped me to see that I am just as worthy of being saved. God sent Hosea to bring Gomer out of her sunken place and He sent me Jacob.

Please understand, I am in no way healed but I am also no longer being held captive by the thoughts in my mind. Jace and I are in therapy now and we are fighting to get our peace and happiness back.

This is why when Jacob asked me to marry him on Christmas, in front of his family, I said yes. We have decided to not have sex until our wedding night, which will be my birthday, May 17, 2018, in Hawaii.

I decided to get married on my birthday as a way to celebrate the new Jayme Walker. The one who is no longer identified as a victim but is acknowledged as a survivor.

Just a word

Although Jayme's story is fictional, there are a lot of women and men who are just like Jayme. Each day you are living with the fear and voices of what molestation, sexual and physical abuse has done to you and taken from you. Many times the abuse is at the hands of someone close to you and you are too afraid to tell it.

Other times, you get the courage to tell and no one believes you. So, you spend the days covering up the hurt and the nights crying yourself to sleep. Or worst, jumping from relationship to relationship and masking the pain with your alcohol or drug of choice.

Beloved, you can and will survive but you have to be willing to get help. It doesn't matter that momma or grandmother didn't believe in therapists, talk to somebody. If not a therapist, confide in someone you trust. And although it is easy to talk to someone who has been through it, it only helps if they have overcame it.

More importantly, pray. Remove the Do Not Disturb sign from your heart and let God in. With Him, He will lead you to someone who can help you. It may not be a Jacob Wallace but it will be somebody strong enough to carry you on the days your legs refuse to move.

It is my hope that you are healed, delivered and set free. If you need prayer, email me at authorlakisha@gmail.com. And if you need help, get it. DO NOT be afraid to ask for help because it could be the very thing that frees you from your sunken place.

Dear God,

Hear the prayer and heal the heart of the young lady or man who needs you now. God, I don't know what fear has robbed them of but I trust you and know you have the power to restore. Do it now Father. Give rest to the person who tosses and turns, all night long. Protect the ones who still has to see their abuser at family functions. Free the voice of the one who is too ashamed to tell it. Surround them with a body of believers who will stand in the gap, fighting for their soul to be freed. Do it now God because we need you to hear their prayer.

Amen.

About the author

Lakisha Johnson, native Memphian and author of ten titles was born to write. She'll tell you that "Writing didn't find me, it's was engraved in my spirit during creation." Along with being an author, she is an ordained minister, co-pastor, wife, mother and the product of a large family. She is an avid blogger at kishasdailydevotional.com and social media poster where she utilizes her gifts to encourage others to tap into their God given talents. She won't claim to be the best at what she does nor does she have all the answers, she is simply grateful to be used by God.

You can connect with Lakisha on:

Facebook: KishaDJohnson | AuthorLakisha

Facebook Group: Twins Write 2

Twitter: @ _kishajohnson

Instagram: kishajohnson

Snapchat: Authorlakisha

Email: authorlakisha@gmail.com

Amazon by searching Lakisha Johnson

ALSO AVAILABLE FROM
LAKISHA

Christian Women's Journal

– Heroine Addict

You are probably asking, why is this journal different from all the rest? After all, it is another book filled with blank pages intended for your thoughts, affirmations, poems, scriptures and etc.; however, this journal was created in the hope you will become addicted to heroine.

No, not the drug but the woman you are and destined to become. The woman who is admired by others, who is held in high regard, who is favorable and filled with courage. The woman who is honorable and of good quality. This journal was created, through prayer, in order to encourage you to search for, find, pull out and then display the heroine within you because your destiny depends on her surviving.

You can order through this link: https://www.paypal.me/AuthorLakisha/15

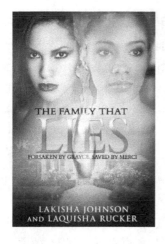

The Family that Lies

Born only months apart, Merci and Grayce Alexander were as close as sisters could get. With a father who thought the world of them, life was good. Until one day everything changed.

While Grayce got love and attention, Merci got all the hell, forcing her to leave home. She never looks back, putting the past behind her until ... her sister shows up over a decade later begging for help, bringing all of the forgotten past with her. Merci wasn't the least bit prepared for what was about to happen next.

Merci realizes, she's been a part of something much bigger than she'd ever imagined. Yea, every family has their secrets, hidden truths and ties but Merci had no idea she'd been born into the family that lies.

https://www.amazon.com/Family-that-Lies-Lakisha-Johnson-ebook/dp/B01MAZD49X

The Pastor's Admin

Daphne 'Dee' Gary used to love being an admin ... until Joseph Thornton. She has been his administrative assistant for ten years and each year, she has to decide whether it will be his secrets or her sanity. And the choice is beginning to take a toil.

Joseph is the founder and pastor of Assembly of God Christian Center and he is, hell, there are so many words Daphne can use to describe him but none are good. He does things without thinking of the consequence because he knows Dee will be there to bail him out. Truth is, she has too because ... it's her job, right? A job she has been questioning lately.

Daphne knows life can be hard and flesh will sometimes win but when she has to choose between HIS SECRETS or HER SANITY, this time, will she remain The Pastor's Admin?

DISCLAIMER This is Christian FICTION which includes some sex scenes and language. ***

https://www.amazon.com/Pastors-Admin-Lakisha-Johnson-ebook/dp/B07B9V4981

Dear God: Hear My Prayer